Obsession 2:

Keeping Secrets

Obsession 2:

Keeping Secrets

Treasure Hernandez

www.urbanbooks.net

Urban Books, LLC
97 N18th Street
Wyandanch, NY 11798

Obsession 2: Keeping Secrets

ISBN 13: 978-1-62286-989-3
ISBN 10: 1-62286-989-3

First Mass Market Printing September 2016
First Trade Paperback Printing November 2014
Printed in the United States of America

10 9 8 7 6 5 4 3 2 1

Distributed by Kensington Publishing Corp.
Submit orders to:
Customer Service
400 Hahn Road
Westminster, MD 21157-4627
Phone: 1-800-733-3000
Fax: 1-800-659-2436

Obsession 2:

Keeping Secrets

Treasure Hernandez

Chapter One

"I don't know why the fuck you sitting there looking out that window; like that sorry-ass motherfucker really gonna come strolling up that walkway," Yolanda spat off to her seventeen-year-old daughter, Secret.

"Ma, please," Secret said, sucking her teeth and rolling her eyes. "Not today. Okay? Dang, if he comes, he comes. If he doesn't, he doesn't. But it doesn't make it any better with you breathing down my neck, hurling all those insults."

"*Hurling,*" Yolanda mocked. "Bitch first one in the family to finish high school and now she using big words like hurling." Yolanda roared out a taunting laugh. "It doesn't matter whether you graduate high school, college, or whatever. You gonna be living right here in the hood like the rest of us. So don't go thinking you all that now that you got a degree."

"Diploma," Secret said under her breath.

"Huh? What was that?" Yolanda questioned, placing her hand to her ear, signaling Secret to speak up. "You think you smart *and* grown? Then if it's like that, if you got something to say, bitch, then say it loud enough for another bitch to hear."

Secret knew it was probably in her best interest to just stay quiet and not repeat herself. There was nothing her mother hated more than being made to feel belittled by having Secret correct her. But how Secret saw it, Yolanda was already on a roll. She was going to pick at her regardless, so she might as well give her something to bitch about.

"I said it's a diploma—a high school diploma— not a degree. A degree is what you get from college."

Secret had already braced herself for the smack before Yolanda's hand had even risen in the air. When it landed on her left cheek, Secret didn't even flinch. She just let off a smirk and turned her attention back toward the window.

"Stupid bitch," Yolanda said, realizing her daughter was immune to all her ranting and raving . . . and now even her physical blows. She'd been beating Secret down with her tongue before the child even came out of her womb. She was just so filled with hate. It wasn't Secret she hated, it was Secret's father, Rolland, a man fifteen years her senior.

When Yolanda got pregnant with Secret she was actually just about Secret's age now. Rolland was her school bus driver. Yolanda was his first and only pick-up and last and only drop-off. In total they only spent about five minutes alone on the bus each weekday. But that's all it took for Rolland to talk the seventeen-year-old into hooking up with him.

Everything started out innocent enough with Rolland playing more the role of a big brother or favorite uncle. He'd lend a listening ear while she talked about high school woes. He'd take her to the movies, out for ice cream, skating, just fun stuff that young girls her age liked to do.

Little things meant a lot to young neighborhood girls like Yolanda, who never had a father in her life to do those types of things with. It was as if every little thing she wanted while they were out she got. No one could have told young Yolanda that Rolland wasn't ballin' after buying her a gold necklace, a purse, a couple outfits, and a pair of Nikes. At first she hid her relationship with Rolland from everybody, including her mother. She came clean when her mother noticed all of her new, nice things, things her single mother couldn't afford and neither could Yolanda, since she wasn't even working at the time.

Young Yolanda was surprised when her mother didn't disapprove of the relationship. She actually cheered Yolanda on to continue the relationship and take it to higher levels. "Hell, the more he buys you, the less I have to," was her mother's theory. "Plus you might as well learn young the power of pussy."

Yolanda's mother's mouth dropped open when Yolanda revealed that it wasn't like that with Rolland, that she hadn't had sex with him, and, in fact, she was still a virgin.

"Oh, so that's what all these gifts are," her mother said. "He was just getting the pussy nice and wet. Prepping you." A grin spread across her lips. "Well, damn, if he got you all that shit just by smelling the pussy, no telling what that nigga gon' break you off when he actually get to run up in it."

Yolanda's mother immediately went and popped in a porn, teaching Yolanda how to give it to Rolland properly. Sometimes a humiliated Yolanda would even have to endure some hands-on demonstrations by her mother.

To make a long story short, Yolanda lost her virginity to Rolland, and when she ended up pregnant, he lost his job. Rumors about Yolanda and Rolland started to surface, and before any truth was discovered, Rolland quit. Yolanda's mother was pissed to say the least. Here she had given this man her underage baby girl on a silver platter so that he could keep her laced with material things, and he went and relinquished his only source of income. But as pissed as Yolanda's mother might have been, nobody was more teed off than Rolland's wife and three kids, about whom he'd never told Yolanda.

Things went from bad to worse. Yolanda's mother put her and her new baby girl out when she realized what she thought would lead to a profit ended up being a deficit. Rolland's wife put him out and his kids turned their back on him, with the help of their mother pounding into their head how sorry their daddy was. The lopsided-in-age couple lived together for a little while in the Section 8 apartment Yolanda got approved for. Rolland tried to make some fast money by trying his hand at the crack game, but ended up getting high off his own supply. Ultimately he chose crack and a life on the streets over Yolanda and their child together, having robbed Yolanda of her youth and her household gadgets such as televisions, then ultimately leaving her and her baby to fend for themselves. For that, a seed of hate was embedded in Yolanda for Rolland that unfortunately trickled down to his seed, their child together, Secret Miller.

"Sit your ass in that window until the fucking end of the world for all I care," Yolanda spat to Secret, picking up her pack of cigarettes from the coffee table and placing one in her mouth. She used the lighter that was tucked down in the outer packaging of the pack to light her cigarette. She then placed the lighter back into its safe haven and threw the pack back down on the table. "But just in case that no-good daddy of yours does show up, make him stop at KFC and buy me some chicken. A two-piece dark. And if you get me that ol' baked shit instead of fried like you did the last time, I'ma bust you upside your muthafuckin' head." Yolanda took a drag, exhaled, then headed down the hall to her bedroom in their two-bedroom apartment. She mumbled, "That's the least that bum owes me for ruining my life," before her door slammed.

Secret jumped when she heard the door nearly come off the hinges. She closed her eyes. She wasn't sure if she was trying to keep the tears in or the pain; both always managed to show themselves through her eyes.

Pain was all she knew: pain from her mother being in her life and pain from her father not being in her life. Funny thing was, she resented her mother more. At least Rolland had the decency to not poison her twenty-four-seven like her mother did. He'd realized that he was a better father out of her life than in it. If only Yolanda could grab hold of that same theory.

How Secret saw it, if Rolland could rescue her from her mother for just five minutes, he was all right by her. Secret had to admit though, over the years she'd waited by that window for him to show up after he'd sworn on a stack of Bibles he'd be there "this time" more times than she could count.

Him being a no-show was worse when Secret was younger, but now, like with her mother, she was immune to it. It hurt, but not so bad anymore.

Secret looked down at her watch, one of the very few things Rolland had ever gotten her. It was almost seven o'clock, six fifty-four to be exact. It hit Secret that she'd been in that window since two o'clock, the original time Rolland had said he'd be there to get her.

"I might run a little late because I have a job interview," Rolland had said on his phone call to Secret earlier that morning, "but I promise you,

Daddy gon' be there. I missed your high school graduation last weekend, but I'm going to make it up to you. I got you a special present."

He had sounded so sincere to Secret's ears. But then again he always had. As the clock struck seven, Secret had to force herself to come to the reality that this was going to be another one of those times when her father didn't show up.

She closed the curtain and stood up. "Guess I better take out some chicken to fry," she said to herself, knowing that Yolanda was going to demand some chicken one way or the other. Secret walked to the kitchen, opened the freezer, and looked around.

"Bingo," she said, eyeing a pack of leg quarters. She picked up the frozen chicken, then closed the refrigerator. She then made her way over to the sink in preparation of filling it with hot water in order to start thawing the chicken. Before she could turn on the water she heard the doorbell ring.

Just as frozen as the chicken that rested in her hands, a glimmer of hope sparkled in Secret's eyes.

Chapter Two

Secret, sure that it was her father at the door, took the chicken and placed it back in the freezer. With a huge smile on her face she ran to the door and flung it wide open. "I knew you would come. . . ." Her words trailed off.

"Well, I ain't had that type of greeting since I showed up on my baby daddy's doorstep wearing nothing but a rain jacket and some red open-toe stilettos." Sissy, their next-door neighbor, laughed. "But anyway, here." She shoved a cup into Secret's hand. "That's the cup your mother let me borrow some sugar in the other day. She raised hell about me not returning her cup. So make sure you let her know I brought it back, with her ol' stingy evil self," Sissy murmured. "But don't tell her I said that. I need to keep her on my good side." She laughed as if she'd just told the funniest joke in the world. "With six kids over there, God only knows what I might need to borrow tomorrow." Sissy winked and trotted off back to the apartment next door.

Secret stared down in the cup. For a minute she thought she might fill it with tears. "You're a big girl now," she coached herself. "Keep it together."

She slowly turned around and began to close the door behind her, but then something blocked it.

"I ain't seen you in all this time and this how you treat me? You just gon' slam the door in your daddy's face?"

Secret looked up to see Rolland standing there, his foot blocking the door to keep it from closing and his arms spread out as wide as the smile on his face, beckoning her for a hug.

"Daddy!" Secret cried out, then collapsed in her father's arms. "I just knew you were coming this time. I just knew it." Secret sniffled back tears of joy. God had answered her prayers. She was about to get some peace from the wrath of Yolanda. Who cared if it was just a couple of hours? It was two hours of peace she otherwise would not have had.

"Baby girl, I told you I was coming." Rolland pulled back from Secret and held her at arm's length. "You're not crying are you?"

"No, Daddy, uh-uh." Secret turned away from her father and wiped her nose with the back of her hand. She blinked away the forming tears in her eyes. "Let me get my purse; then we can go."

Just as Secret headed down the hallway to her room Yolanda's door opened. She came out holding a cigarette between her fingers, patting her hair into place. Although a few minutes ago she'd been wearing a hot pink jogging suit, she was now clad in a short nightgown with a pink robe that was deliberately untied.

Secret stopped before heading into her room. She gave her mother the once-over. "I see you changed into something more comfortable." It was apparent Yolanda had obviously heard Secret shout out that her father was there and did a quick change. Perhaps she was trying to get with her father. Maybe she was just trying to tease Rolland, show him what he was missing out on. Either way, Secret was disgusted. She shook her head then headed to her room to grab her purse.

"Yolanda, you looking good," Rolland said, rubbing his hands together and licking his lips.

"Nigga, go on somewhere with that bullshit," Yolanda said. "You know I've always looked good." She cracked a smile and then walked into the living room where Rolland stood, waiting for his daughter.

"You right about that," Rolland agreed.

Yolanda just stood there for a minute eye-balling Rolland up and down. "You ain't looking too bad yourself. You ain't on that shit no more are you? Because I don't want you having my daugh—"

"All right, Dad. I'm ready," Secret said as she came bouncing out of her room like she was a seven-year-old instead of seventeen.

For some reason, whenever her father did come around, it was like she regressed to the little girl he left behind all those years ago. It was a telltale sign of her longing to be daddy's little girl.

"Then let's go," Rolland said, clapping his hands together.

He did not have to tell Secret twice, as she was already halfway out the door.

"You take care of yourself, Yolanda," Rolland said, backpedaling.

"Umm, hmm, Rolland." Yolanda bit the bottom of her lip in a sexy, teasing manner. "Maybe when you drop Secret off you can come in and maybe we can share a little nightcap or something. You know, like old times." Yolanda was trying her hardest not to let the desperate look show through her eyes as she painted on a smile to cover it up.

"Maybe," Rolland said, turning and walking away before throwing another, "Maybe," over his shoulder.

"Maybe?" Yolanda said under her breath. "Bitch throwing pussy at you like this and yo' ass talking about some maybe?" Yolanda held her middle finger up and mumbled under her breath, "Fuck you, Rolland Miller. Fuck you!" before slamming the door closed.

"So where are we going, Dad?" Secret asked as she and Rolland drove out of her Flint, Michigan neighborhood. "Oh, and what about the graduation present you said you had for me?" Secret looked in the back seat hoping to see a beautifully wrapped graduation present sitting in the back. All she saw were empty beer cans, some McDonald's trash, and a couple CD cases. She turned back around, disappointed.

"Oh, don't worry, baby girl," Rolland said after looking over and seeing the disappointment on his daughter's face. "Daddy got you. Matter of fact, we 'bout to make this stop and then we gon' go get your present. I promise." Rolland patted Secret's knee.

Secret looked over at her father and smiled, then looked down at her knee that he was still patting almost subconsciously. She politely removed his hand from her leg.

"Oh, my bad," Rolland said with just a hint of nervousness behind his tone. He seemed so preoccupied and uptight about something. "So how was graduation? Did you graduate with summa cum laude or something? I know you did, as smart as you are."

"Graduation was good. No, I didn't graduate summa cum laude, but my grades were pretty good." Secret thought about how hard she'd worked to maintain an A average all throughout high school. Not going to college was not an option, so she sacrificed her high school years hitting the books instead of having fun and hitting the streets like most of her peers. "I'm still waiting to hear back about this scholarship I applied for. If it comes through, I plan on moving to Ohio and go to Ohio State University. Just to get away, you know."

"Oh, no, you can't become a Buckeye. Folks here will skin you alive when you come back to visit if you go attend school at their biggest rival university in history."

Secret laughed at her father's exaggeration. "Dad, you crazy, but I just think OSU will be perfect. It's not too far, but far enough to get away from . . ." Secret's words trailed off.

"From that mother of yours," Rolland leaned in and said in a whisper.

Secret just smiled and shrugged, her way of saying yes without actually verbalizing it.

"Trust me, I understand. That's why I had to leave her."

Secret's smiled faded. "But you didn't just leave her. You left me too," Secret said almost as if she'd been waiting for an opportunity to say that to her father.

There was brief silence in the car as Rolland just looked ahead while driving. Finally he said the words, "You are absolutely right and I'm sorry."

Secret exhaled at Rolland's last two words. *I'm sorry.* That's all she'd ever wanted to hear her father say. It would mean that he acknowledged that he was wrong, and not that something was wrong with her. Because for years she had wondered if she had anything to do with her father's disappearing act. Had she done something wrong? Now she knew nothing was wrong with her. Rolland's leaving was on him and not about her. And then of course Yolanda had her part in it. Secret couldn't half blame him for wanting to get as far away from her mother as possible. After all, that was her ultimate goal as well. The Ohio State University would have to be far enough.

Secret turned to look at her father as he continued talking.

"At the time, when I left your mother, I didn't even look at it as if I was walking out on you too. Daddy had so much going on in life. I was messed up, baby girl," he said, shaking his head. "I was messed up and I messed up. And, baby, I am soo soo sorry. Daddy means that from the bottom of his heart." This time he just rested his hand on her knee without all the tapping. "And I'm sorry. Will you forgive me?"

Secret didn't even care if the tears that filled her eyes fell. She was overjoyed with her father's long-overdue apology. "Yes, Daddy, I forgive you." Secret placed her hand on top of her father's. "I forgive you."

Rolland looked at his weeping daughter and almost shed a tear himself, but he quickly gained his composure and looked dead on as he drove. "Just know that I'll do anything for you, Secret, anything at all."

Secret looked over at her father and into his eyes. She had eyes like him. No matter how much he had been or had not been in her life, he was her blood. They were a part of each other. Just this thought alone tugged at her heart.

"Daddy," Secret said after Rolland had directed his attention back to the road.

"Yes, baby girl," he said, busting a sharp right.

"I'll do anything for you too."

Rolland was so moved that he dang near slowed the car down to a complete stop. He turned and faced Secret. Rubbing her cheek with the back of his hand he said, "Secret, you have no idea how glad I am to hear you say that."

Secret simply smiled, ignorant of the underlying meaning of Rolland's words.

Chapter Three

A curious look appeared on Secret's face as her father steered the car down a dark alley. "Daddy, where are we going?" she asked, looking around.

"Oh, uh, yeah, baby," Rolland stammered, "this is where I said I had to stop off first before we go get your graduation present. I was thinking we'd go grab a bite to eat as well." Rolland drove down the alley at a snail's pace, squinting his eyes as if he was looking for something . . . or someone. "You hungry?"

"Yeah," Secret said, no longer focusing on her suspect surroundings as a thought popped in her head. "Oh, and Mama is hungry too. She wants us to bring her back something to eat."

Rolland didn't reply as he hit the brakes.

"What are we stopping in the middle of a dark alley for?" Secret asked, slightly paranoid. She then noticed a dark figure in the headlights. At first she didn't know what to think, if they were about to get robbed, carjacked, or what. But when Rolland started to roll his window down, Secret eased up a little bit, figuring he must be someone her father knew.

"What up, blood?" Rolland said to the dude right before they gave each other some dap.

"Same ol', same ol'," the guy replied. He then bent down and took a look at Secret. "What's up, pretty girl?" he said, showing his teeth, mostly blinged out.

Secret just nodded. She didn't like the way the man was looking at her, like he was undressing her with his eyes, so she quickly looked away toward her father. "Daddy, I'm ready to go get something to eat." Secret hoped her father caught on to the fact that that was code for, "Let's get the hell out of here; this dude is creeping me out."

"Yeah, yeah, in minute, baby girl," Rolland told his daughter without taking his eyes off his friend.

"If you hungry, I got you, pretty girl," Rolland's friend said to Secret. "As a matter of fact, I think I have just what you like." He looked at Rolland. "So what's up? What time you gon' come back? A couple of hours?" He looked over at Secret and then licked his lips. "Matter of fact, make it three. And don't worry, I'll hook you up with a little somethin'-somethin' extra."

"Daddy," Secret said, tensing up. "Let's go. I . . . I just want to go home." Secret didn't hide the fact that she was scared. She felt as if she was part of a plan that she knew nothing about, yet the plan involved her.

"Hold up, baby girl." Rolland turned his body as much as he could in his seat to face Secret. "Remember when you said you'd do anything for Daddy? Well, baby, right now I really need you to make good on your word." He squirmed a little. "You see Daddy is having it real hard right now. I been off that stuff a little bit now, but you know I did that bid in jail, too."

Secret didn't know exactly which bid he was talking about. He'd done several. As a matter of fact, that's one of the reasons why he'd been out of her life so much, because he was in jail so much.

"I just need you to do me this one solid. Please, Secret, and I promise I won't ever ask you to do anything like this again." He nodded over his shoulder to the man standing outside the window. Then in a whispered tone he said, "Just a couple hours with him and I swear to—"

"Daddy, no!" Secret yelled out, her eyes filling with tears. "How could you?" She turned to try to get out of the car but Rolland stopped her by grabbing her arm.

"Just wait, Secret. Please, Daddy needs you to do this."

Secret just sat there trembling with fear, tears rolling down her face.

"Look, keepin' it one hun'id; Daddy owes some really bad people a lot of money. If I don't pay them, baby girl, you probably won't ever see your daddy again . . . alive that is. And I ain't just talking shit either, Secret. They gon' kill your daddy if I don't get them their money." Rolland fought back tears of his own.

Secret just sat there shaking her head. "Daddy, how could you? How could you ask your daughter to . . ." She couldn't even say it, let alone ever imagining doing it.

Rolland exhaled. "I know. You're right. I don't know what I was thinking. This is crazy. I was just desperate. I was just trying to get my life back together so that I could be a better man, be a better father to you." He buried his face in his hands. "Will you forgive me, baby girl? Oh God, will you forgive me?" He cried as his shoulders heaved up and down.

Secret's chest was rising up and down. She was plagued with fear, sorrow, disappointment, betrayal, and disbelief. As she looked at her father, she started to feel sorry for him as well.

On top of all that, she was feeling confused. She'd already forgiven her father once today. She never saw it coming that she'd be having to forgive him again, and so soon.

"Look, it ain't going down," Rolland turned and said to the guy.

The dude raised his hands in the air, his facial expression questioning what was going on. "Man, what the fuck? How you gon' play me? How you gon' set this shit up, get my dick all hard"—he grabbed his manhood—"and then say some bullshit-ass 'it ain't going down'?"

"Look, I made a mistake. I fucked up," Rolland told the guy. "Sorry." He then rolled the window up and very slowly proceeded to drive off.

Secret exhaled. She was just so happy to be out of that situation that she was more glad than mad at her father right now. At least he'd come to his senses on the matter.

"I'm so sorry, baby girl." Rolland began to cry. "I feel so ashamed I want to die. I should just kill myself." Rolland began beating his head on the steering wheel repeatedly while yelling out, "Stupid! Stupid! Stupid! I'm so stupid! I deserve to die anyway. I don't even deserve to be in your life."

"Daddy, stop. Please stop." Secret reached over and grabbed her father to keep him from slamming his head into the steering wheel again. "Daddy, don't hurt yourself like that."

"Why? I'm going to be dead by the morning anyway. I might as well kill myself, 'cause they gon' kill me anyway." He looked into his daughter's eyes. "Secret, they gon' kill your daddy." Rolland began to cry harder, snot running out of his nose and everything.

Secret became so emotional that she wrapped her arms around her father and began to cry just as hard as he was. She hated seeing him like this. The way he looked, he was already dead. And how Secret saw it, his blood would be on her hands. How would she be able to live with herself? On the other hand, her father had been anything but father of the year. He didn't deserve for her to sacrifice herself just to save him. But then she thought about the message that preacher had taught a couple months ago when her best friend, Shawndiece, invited her to Friends and Family Day at her cousin's church. The family who brought the most people to church got a free dinner, which was the only reason why Shawndiece even set foot in the church. Secret had gone to church lots of times with her grandmother. As far as she was concerned, her mother might as well have been Satan himself, so no way did they ever go to church together.

That preacher at Shawdiece's cousin's church had spoken about how no one on earth had deserved it, yet Jesus had sacrificed His life for them. *And look what happened to Him.*

"Daddy, stop the car," Secret said.

"Huh? What?" Rolland asked.

"I said stop the car." Looking straight ahead Secret said, "Go back."

Rolland put his foot on the brake. "Do . . . do you really mean it?" Rolland could hardly keep himself in check. He would have jumped in the air and clicked his heels together if he could have.

"Please, Daddy. Just turn the car around before I change my mind," Secret said, closing her eyes and swallowing hard.

Rolland was all too quick to wipe his drying tears away, put a smirk on his face, and throw the car in reverse.

Secret tried to think of how Jesus was now sitting at the right hand of God up in heaven for the sacrifice He'd made. Secret knew she was no Jesus, but what she did know was that like Jesus, she'd have to go through hell first in order to get to heaven.

Chapter Four

"Don't be scared," the man who Secret had first seen in the headlights of her father's car said to her. Now they were no longer in a dark alley, but in a Cape Cod–style home.

After her father had let her out of the car, promising he'd be right there in that alley waiting for her once she was finished handling her business, the man had led Secret through a gate, up a pathway, and into the back door of the home. Upon entering the house, she was greeted by a candlelit table set for two. There was a spread of food: fried chicken, mashed potatoes and gravy, macaroni and cheese, biscuits, and a chocolate cake with white icing drizzling down it. Under closer observation, Secret realized the meal was compliments of KFC. Her mother ate it so much, she'd know their food anywhere.

"See, told you if you were hungry I got you," the man said, extending his hand toward the food. "I even got you some of this." He walked over to the table and pulled out a bottle of Moscato from a silver-tin bucket filled with ice that was resting in between the candles. His smile was a mile wide and reeked of pride. "Umm, hmm, you like that don't you? Your boy is on point, huh?"

"I'm not old enough to drink," Secret said, raining on his parade.

His smile turned upside down as he placed the bottle back into its resting place. He thought for a moment and then rushed over to the refrigerator. "Ta-da." He beamed, pulling out a half-empty two liter of Tahitian Treat. "Just cracked it open for lunch today. It should still have most of its fizz."

Secret could tell that the man seemed to be trying hard to impress her, only she couldn't reciprocate his enthusiasm. Not being enthused was an understatement.

"So, have a seat." He pulled out a chair for Secret.

"Thank you, but I'm not hungry. I just want to get this over with." Secret didn't say the words nasty or mean or anything. She really did just want to get it over. She was five seconds from turning around and running out of that door. She considered the fact that Rolland had pretty much been dead in her life anyway since he never really came around. What would be the difference if he really did end up dead?

But before the five seconds was up, the man approached Secret and began kissing on her. His tongue felt like that of a slithering snake. There was no way she could get into this, because a snake was a snake and eventually she knew it would bite. She could feel his hands, tongue, and other parts of his body taking over hers right there in the kitchen. It was as if she'd already been bitten and now the poison had paralyzed her and she couldn't move. She couldn't do anything but stand there and allow the snake to eat her alive.

At least maybe now I will be immune to a man's venom . . . I mean a snake's, Secret thought. But that's about as much detail as there was. Once Secret felt her clothing being removed, it was now like she was the snake, shedding her skin. So not only was her clothing, her skin, being removed, so was her soul. So she removed herself mentally as well. This would be the discovery of a characteristic Secret would find herself having to use often in life.

Her thoughts fast-forwarded to her running out to the mailbox and finding a letter stating that she'd received a full ride to college.

She imagined packing up and heading off to Columbus, Ohio on the Greyhound, where her new dorm and the best and most fun roommate in the world would await her. She'd live the life a college freshmen should live, cramming for midterms and finals all week while partying on the weekends.

"Was you a virgin or something?"

The man's question pulled Secret from her daydreams back to reality. Reality was him standing over her, looking down at his wet penis. The coldness from the kitchen floor on her bare backside gave her chills. She sat up, bringing her knees to her chest and hugging her arms around them.

"Or was you on your period or something?" he asked. "Because there's blood on my shit." He grabbed a napkin from off the kitchen table and began wiping himself.

"Both," Secret said nonchalantly.

"Motherfucker," he said as he turned and headed down the bathroom, fussing and cussing the entire time.

Secret couldn't help but to let out a chuckle. She wasn't really on her period. She'd already had it last week. She just wanted to gross him out. Looked like it had worked. She was a virgin though, which was why she forced herself to mentally escape while he was having sex with her. She knew it would hurt and she didn't want to experience the pain. At least not while he was penetrating her. But as she sat there on the floor, gathering her clothing, she could feel it now.

Secret heard the water running in the bathroom and figured the man, whose name she never bothered to ask, was cleaning himself up. What did she need to know his name for? If there was a God, she'd never have to see the likes of him ever again.

A few minutes later, after Secret had gotten herself dressed, the man came back into the kitchen.

"Here, it's all there." He handed her an envelope.

"What's this?" Secret asked, taking the envelope.

"It's your old man's money," he replied. "I don't know how y'all gon' split that up, but this one is just for you." He proceeded to hand Secret another envelope. "It's an extra G." He put his head down. "What you gave me was special. I figure the least I can do is give you a little something extra."

Secret didn't know what to say, so she said nothing.

After a few moments of silence, the man walked over and opened the door. "I'll walk you out."

"No, thank you," Secret said. "I'm good."

"Indeed you are," the man said. "And if you ever need anything"—he grazed Secret's chin with his index finger—"you know where to find me. I'm sure we can work something out—you know, some type of barter and trade." He winked.

Secret looked down and turned to exit. Before walking out the door she turned to the man and said, "As a matter of fact, there is something I need."

When Secret entered her apartment, Yolanda was sitting on the couch, smoking a cigarette. "Let me see what that cheap-ass bastard got you for your graduation," Yolanda said.

Secret thought for a minute. "Oh, I, uh, left it in his car," she lied. She wasn't about to tell her mother that her father hadn't even managed to get her a graduation present. Yolanda would run with that for months, reminding Secret every chance she got how she wasn't even worthy of her own father buying her a gift.

"Well, what was it?"

Secret had to think quickly on her feet. "Just a couple things for when I go off to college."

"Humph," Yolanda said. She took a puff of her cigarette and then just looked at Secret, who was standing there, silent, her head down. "What the fuck wrong with you? Over there looking like you just lost your best friend or something."

"Nothing, I'm good. Just tired. I'm going to go take a shower and go to bed." Secret headed toward her bedroom. Even if she and her mother had the Clair and Denise Huxtable mother-daughter type of relationship, what she'd just experienced wasn't something she felt like sitting down to chop it up about. She never wanted to think about it again, let alone talk about it. She just wanted to go take a shower, go to bed, and then wake up to another day in the hood, counting toward the day she'd get out of the hood.

"What's that in your hand?"

Secret stopped in her tracks and looked down at the foil-covered plate. She'd forgotten all about it and that she was even holding it. "Oh, yeah, I almost forgot." She walked over to where Yolanda was sitting and extended the plate to her.

Yolanda snatched it and began to unwrap it. Inside were four pieces of KFC and some sides. Before leaving the guy's house, Secret had asked him if it was okay if she made a plate to go. He obliged her by telling her to take all that she wanted. Afterward, she walked out to Rolland's car, which was parked in the exact same spot in the alley as when she'd left it.

When she got in she just handed him the envelope. The two didn't even make eye contact. There was no way Secret could look into her father's eyes knowing he knew the deed she'd just done. She'd just given her body to a man. Even though it was her father who had handed her to the man on a silver platter, she still felt like a cheap $9.99 all-you-can-eat buffet.

Even when Secret handed her father the envelope the man had given her, he opened his mouth to start to say "thank you" to her, but then closed it when he realized that no words were ever going to come out. Secret imagined there was nothing he could possibly say anyway to take away the worthless feeling that was polluting her thoughts. Even when he pulled up in front of Secret's apartment to drop her off, there was no good-bye. As Secret walked up her walkway, she knew she'd never see Rolland again. The irony of it all; he was as good as dead.

"Good, it's fried. Not that baked shit," Yolanda said, picking up a piece of chicken and taking a bite.

Secret headed toward her bedroom

"What you want me to do? Eat this with my goddamn fingers?"

Secret made a detour to the kitchen, grabbed her mother a fork, and then walked it back to her. Yolanda took it and dug right into the macaroni and cheese.

Before Secret started her trek to her bedroom yet again, she remembered something else. She reached down in her purse and pulled out the other envelope the man had given her to keep. She threw it on the couch next to Yolanda, then turned and walked to her bedroom.

"What's this?" Yolanda said with a mouthful of food.

"It's compliments of Dad. I guess you could say back child support," she said before going in her room and closing the door behind her.

Chapter Five

"Man, nigga, maybe if you stop fucking all them crackheads, you won't have to be down at the free clinic every other month," Lucky said to his boy, Major Pain.

"Nigga, fuck you," Major Pain replied. "It ain't even like that. I ain't having no symptoms or nothing like that. It's just that my shit ain't felt right since I fucked this one broad a couple weeks ago. I just want to make sure I'm good. I don't want no syphilis or some shit like that lingering in my dick. You know that shit can make you go blind if you let it go untreated."

"If you ain't went blind from all that jacking off you do to all them pornos, then you ain't never going blind." Lucky began to laugh harder.

"You real funny," Major Pain said as they walked up the steps leading to the clinic's door. "You got mad jokes."

"I'd rather have jokes than crabs," Lucky said, taking one last shot at his partner.

The two friends laughed, always going tit for tat at one another. Lucky and Major Pain had met through the city's top and most ruthless drug dealer named Turf. Before Lucky had ever even met Major Pain, his reputation had preceded him, known for his wild, violent, "I don't give a fuck about nobody and nothing" attitude. But he was paid, taking out niggas left and right for the sake of Team Turf. Lucky had just started putting in work for Turf at the time, but knew if he handled his business, he, too, could develop the same attitude as Major Pain, leading to him being just as paid as him as well.

With getting paid as his ultimate goal, it was easy for Lucky to take on that same type of "I don't give a fuck" mentality as well. That attitude led to him killing Ivy, the girlfriend of his best friend at the time, Quick. Lucky claimed it was an accident, but because of the "get money" and "money over bitches" attitude, he never knew if Quick ever truly believed him. And he never would know because Quick and the new girl he got with, Tiffany, would end up dead, gunned down by the police. That shitty-ass cop, Detective Davis, wouldn't rest until he saw the squad dead or in jail. Lucky had been just that: lucky not to have fallen victim to any of Davis's efforts.

Lucky and Major Pain would now have something else in common, seeing that Major Pain had lost his best friend, Wolf, in a shootout. The two last soldiers standing would become partners in crime, literally.

"So why all the chicks I get down with gotta be crackheads?" Major Pain shot back. "I mean, your mama don't look like a crackhead to me." He held his stomach with laughter.

"Nigga, fuck you," Lucky said seriously as he opened the door to the clinic. Mama jokes always brought the back-and-forth banter to a halt for some reason.

The two walked inside. "Yo, man, I'ma sit my black ass right out here in the lobby," Lucky said.

"Just come on back here with me." Major Pain nodded toward the next set of doors that led to the sign-in desk. "You know I'ma be waiting forever. You might as well come back and kick it with me."

"And look like I'm yo' bitch or something? Mu'fucka, you better play with your iPhone . . . or your dick for that matter. I'll be right here waiting after you get your penicillin shot." Lucky laughed, flopping down in a chair.

"Fuck you," were Major Pain's parting words as he headed back to sign in with the receptionist.

Lucky picked up a pamphlet and began to read about birth control, which had a message that abstinence was the best form of birth control. "Yeah, and that shit is the best way to get blue balls, too," Lucky said to himself, throwing the pamphlet back down on the table. He heard a chime letting him know he'd just gotten a text. He pulled his phone out of his jacket pocket, read it, and began texting back.

"Damn, he fine as hell," Lucky heard a female voice say. He was the only one in the lobby, so he knew the person must have been referring to him. He was finishing up a text though and wanted to get it sent without error, so he didn't bother looking up.

"Yeah, girl, but are you forgetting where you at?" another female voice said lowly.

"True. He got a dirty dick."

Both girls burst out laughing and that's when Lucky looked up to see them heading toward the exit door. They'd obviously just come from the registration/treatment area and were now leaving.

"You in the same place I am," Lucky finally spoke. "Does that mean you got a dirty pussy?"

Both girls looked at Lucky then burst out laughing, continuing to make their way outside.

Ordinarily Lucky might have been pissed off enough to call the girls all kinds of bitches and hoes. But not this time. There was something about the way one of the girls looked at him that let him know she was far from a bitch or a ho. Her soft brown eyes delivered a sense of innocence and purity. Her soft-looking lips polished with pink lip gloss looked as if they spoke of nothing but sweet dreams. Lucky had to admit that she was the first girl to ever render him speechless.

By the time Lucky awoke from the hypnotic state her eyes had seemed to put him in, both girls were out the door. The playa in Lucky told him to let them go, but his curiosity was piqued. He had to know what he might be missing.

"Yo, ladies, hold up," Lucky said after jumping up out of his seat in the lobby and catching up with the girls outside.

"Girl, just keep walking," he could hear one of them say under her breath to the other. "Remember: dirty dick."

"Uh, just in case you didn't know, I can hear y'all talking about me back here," Lucky spoke up, as he stayed on the girls' heels.

The girls looked at each other, giggled, but kept walking.

"Yo', y'all gon' stop, slow down, or something?" Lucky asked. "A nigga trying to holler at ya."

One girl stopped in her tracks, spun around, and put her hand on her hip. "Dude, you were in the clinic. Like you said back there, we were in the clinic too. For all we know, everybody's shit is burning up in this bitch. Why you bothering us?"

"'Cause your girl was looking kind of sexy back there," Lucky said, referring to the one who had stopped but had not turned around. She was the one he'd locked eyes with back inside the clinic lobby.

"That's exactly why your ass is up in the clinic now; talkin' 'bout some sexy." The girl looked Lucky up and down. "You fine and all, but ain't no dick worthy of dying over. Bring her your paper that reads you negative, and then y'all can talk. Other than that, have a blessed mutha-fuckin' day." And on that note, the girl spun back around, linked her arm through her friend's, and trotted off again.

Lucky just stood there feeling a certain kind of way: lightweight offended, but intrigued at the same time. He had ninety-nine problems but a bitch had never been one. Broads came and went. But what was it about this particular one? Was it because she wasn't like all the other broads who would drop to their knees and suck his dick in the middle of the street just because he was ballin'?

Most chicks in the streets knew who Lucky was. They knew the whole deal about him working for Turf at one point, then getting put on by Sosa, who was Turf's enemy. Both Sosa and Turf eventually got cuffed and Turf got sent off to prison for damn near the rest of his life. Sosa had to lay low so that he wouldn't endure the same fate as Turf, so he turned over the keys and throne to Lucky. A whole lot went down with the death of Quick, who had taken over Turf's throne and eventually merged with Lucky. At the end of the day, it was now Lucky and Major Pain who were running shit. Women knew that and were always trying to jump on their dicks. But Lucky could tell from just looking in this chick's eyes that she was of an entirely different caliber from those other females. She wasn't like all the other women he'd encountered. She looked like that kind of chick who would have a nigga wanna do the right thing . . . make a baller want to put away his ball and be up under her ass all the time. So as bad as Lucky wanted to step to her, he knew she was exactly the kind of girl a guy like him was better off leaving alone.

Chapter Six

"I ain't 'bout to trip over no bitch and be chasing bitches down and shit," Lucky told himself as he watched the mysterious girl and her friend walk away. They looked over their shoulders at him every now and then and giggled.

As the distance grew between them, Lucky still couldn't help contemplating whether to go and try to get her number. He had a couple options. He could either go back inside the clinic, wait for Major Pain, and end up meeting some hood rat who would give him a real reason to have his ass up in the clinic. He could go back inside the clinic and have visions of that chick in his mind, fucking with his attention span and day-to-day activities. Or he could just go see what was up with her and be done with it.

Figuring it was gon' be what it was gon' be, Lucky headed in the direction of the girls. Once he saw them clear the corner and they were no longer in sight, he started a light jog until he was only a few feet behind them. He watched as they approached the bus stop and sat down on the bench.

"I never pegged you as the type who would be riding the bus," Lucky said to the girl who had caught his eye. "You look all sweet and spoiled; like a daddy's girl or something." Lucky chuckled. "I'm surprised your daddy ain't got you riding around here in a hot ride he got you for your sweet sixteen, graduation, or something."

"Dude really?" the more talkative girl said to Lucky. "We black and we live in the hood. What's the odds of either one of us having a daddy?"

"Look, does your girl talk or do you just like to talk? Because you're the only voice I keep hearing, yet it's not the voice I'm trying to hear. No offense."

"Well, damn, Dirty Dick. I guess you told me," she said, bobbing her head.

"And my name is not Dirty Dick. It's Lucky. And for your information, I'm not at the clinic for myself. I'm there with a friend."

"Yeah, tell us anything." She rolled her eyes.

Finally, her friend spoke. "He was sitting in the lobby, Shawn."

The two girls looked at each other. Their expressions gave off a look that perhaps they believed Lucky was telling the truth.

"Lucky, huh." The girl he'd been chasing after spoke again. "I'm Secret, Secret Miller." She extended her hand.

She was like a princess. Lucky didn't know whether to shake her hand, kiss her hand, or ask for it in marriage. "Pleased to meet you, Secret." He opted to shake her hand. He didn't want to look corny as hell with his other options. He then looked at her friend. "And I know you ain't a secret. You talk too damn much." Before anybody could get an attitude, Lucky started laughing while extending his hand to the girl. "Naw, you know I'm just kidding . . . Shawn?" At least Lucky thought that's what Secret had just called her.

"My friends call me Shawn." She held out her hand and shook Lucky's. "So you can call me by my name, Shawndiece."

"Oh, okay. So it's like that, Shawndiece?" Lucky exaggerated her name.

"Yep, that is until I figure out if you really are lucky, or just bad news like most of the cats around here. Niggas don't seem to want to do nothing with they life but ball or get bitches. Well, I ain't having that for my girl Secret."

Her words shook Lucky for a minute, as Shawndiece had basically just described Lucky to a tee.

"You'll have to excuse her," Secret jumped in, "My girl here is kind of like Bambi from *Basketball Wives LA*. She looks out for her friends for real-for real."

Lucky nodded. "I can respect that. Everybody needs a friend like that."

"Word," Shawndiece agreed.

"So, Lucky, what is it that we can do for you?" Secret asked. "I mean, you did just follow us a half a mile. You must want something."

Lucky was in a trance as Secret inflicted that look in her eyes upon him.

"Earth to Mr. Lucky." Shawndiece was snapping her fingers in front of Lucky's face.

"Oh, my bad. I just wanted to holler at you," he said to Secret. "Tell you how beautiful you are . . ." He paused for a moment, searching for his next words. Had it been any other broad Lucky would have straight-out said, "I wanna fuck wit' you." But he didn't need to be reminded that this wasn't any other girl. "And I just wanted to know if I could maybe get your number and call you sometime."

Secret looked over at Shawndiece as if she was seeking the answer from her. Her eyes were pleading, "Girl, what should I do?"

Shawndiece poked out her lips, folded her arms, and rolled her eyes as she turned away from the couple to look and see if the bus was coming. This was the first time she decided to preserve her voice.

"Well, I uh . . ." Secret stammered.

Not about to be shot down and made a fool of, Lucky went into his pockets and pulled out a receipt he had. "Tell you what; I'm going to give you my number. Do you have a pen?"

Secret began to dig in her purse for a pen, all the while still shooting Shawndiece, who was still ignoring her, a questioning look. Once she finally came across one, she handed it to Lucky.

Lucky wrote down his cell number on the back of the receipt. He then handed both the receipt and pen to Secret. "If you want to, call me sometime. If not, just save the number and remember me as the one who got away, because if I don't hear from you, that's exactly who I'm going to remember you as." On that note Lucky walked away, hoping that for once his name actually meant something and that Secret would call.

Chapter Seven

"Really, Secret," Shawndiece scolded her friend as they sat at the bus stop. "Did you really just take some dude's number who you just met up in the free clinic?" Shawndiece burst out laughing. "Now that takes the cake!" Tears formed in her eyes she was laughing so hard. "I know some chicks be trippin' off the fact that they don't want to meet their soul mate up in no club, but the free clinic, Secret?"

Secret chuckled somewhat. "Now it ain't that funny, Shawndiece." She rolled her eyes.

"Girl, I don't know what you are talking about, but that shit is hilarious to me. I mean, just imagine that you do decide to call Mr. Lucky, the two of you kick it, fall madly in love with each other, get married, and have babies, and y'all's babies have babies. What you gon' tell your grandkids when they grow up and say, 'Nana, how did you and Paw Paw meet?'" Shawndiece stood up, then bent over, pointing her finger while she spoke. "Now listen here, babies," she said, disguising her voice to sound like that of an elderly woman. "Back when I was coming up there was this place called the free clinic. It was where all the fellas with dirty dicks hung out."

Secret laughed and play slapped her best friend on the arm to make her stop.

Shawndiece laughed and sat down, coming out of her grandma character. "You know that ain't gonna make no damn sense. But we won't have to worry about that because I know you ain't even gon' think of calling ol' boy."

Secret ignored Shawdiece's comment while she leaned out to see if the bus was coming.

"Right, Secret?" Shawndiece pressed.

Secret thought about it for a second and then shrugged.

"Girl, please tell me that you are not even thinking about calling that dude." She allowed her eyeballs to roll all over Secret before saying, "Especially not with the predicament that you're in."

Secret wrapped her arms around herself and turned away.

"Look, Secret, I'm not trying to be funny or throw a dig at you, but, girlfriend, you have too much you need to be taking care of with yourself than to be worrying about some thug."

"Why does he have to be a thug?" Secret smiled shyly.

"I don't know; because the streets made him that way probably."

"You know what I meant." Secret rolled her eyes. "How do you know he's a thug? He seemed like a pretty nice guy. I mean a thug would have been calling us all kinds of B-words and whores if we'd ignored him like we did Lucky."

Shawndiece just sat there and stared at Secret for a moment as if she was trying to figure something out. "Even though you and I are like oil and water, I can see why God mixed us together. You need me in your life for real."

"Oh, really?"

"Yeah, I mean, you book smart and all, but that's where it stops. The fact that you are giving that dude the benefit of the doubt, even though he had t-h-u-g stamped on his forehead, shows me that you are just as naïve as everyone says you are, which is probably how ol' dude got you out of your panties in the first place; hence us having to be up at the damn clinic in the second place." Shawndiece was getting a little serious and perturbed at her friend at the same time.

"You ain't 'bout that life, Secret. You can't roll with no street cat like that. You ain't built that way. It would be foreign to you. Girl, you don't even speak the language. Hell, you barely can hang with my ghetto ass."

Friends since the summer Secret and her mother moved into the neighborhood eight years ago, Shawndiece has always been there for Secret. She's always had her back and kept it one hun'id with her.

"I can tell right now you are gonna need me to show you the ropes around here," Shawndiece had said to Secret all those years ago after knowing her for only ten minutes. She'd been walking by Secret's apartment building on the way over to one of her school friend's house. When Secret greeted her with this happy-go-lucky smile and wave, she knew off the bat Secret didn't fit in.

"You're not from here, are you?" Shawndiece asked the new girl on the block.

"Nope, we just moved to the city. I used to live with my grandma in Farmington." Farmington was a suburb in Detroit. "But she died. My mother thought she was going to leave us the house since we lived there with her and all, but she left it to Aunt Grace. Mama says Aunt Grace had that house on the market before Granny was even in the grave. So we had to relocate."

Shawndiece scrunched her nose up.

"We had to move," Secret clarified.

"So now y'all slumming," ten-year-old Shawn-diece said while giving the pretty-in-pink, long-piggy-tail-wearing new girl the once-over.

"Excuse me?" Ten-year-old Secret was clue-less as to what the rough-around-the-edges girl with the holey jeans and French-braided hair with beads on the end was saying.

"I'm saying you came down off your high horse to rub elbows with us little people."

Secret scrunched her nose up. "I don't be riding horses. Although my dad did say he might get me a pony."

Shawndiece busted out laughing. "A pony? You gon' need a pit bull or something if you plan on living here." Shawndiece laughed again.

Secret joined in on the laughter just because.

"You have no idea what you're even laughing at do you?"

Secret's laughter immediately ceased as she shook her head.

"I think I'm gonna like you." She looked Secret up and down. "Even though I can tell we ain't nothing alike, you're honest. My mama says honesty is hard to come by; that people will dog you out, lie on you, and sell you off the *first chance they get and then lie about it." She looked Secret in the eyes. "You don't lie do you?"*

Secret shook her head. "Nope. My granny said you get in less trouble when you tell the truth than you do when you tell a lie."

"Oh, yeah? Well my granny said if you just tell the truth in the first place, you don't have to try to keep up with a lie. And that's how dumb-ass niggas like my Uncle Bobie get caught up."

Secret's eyes grew as big as saucers. "You just cussed and you said the N-word."

"You ain't never heard nobody cuss or say nigga? Don't you listen to rap music?"

"My mama cusses a lot! And she says the N-word. But kids aren't supposed to talk like that."

"Well, Secret, let me let you in on a little . . . secret," Shawndiece said. "These little ashy crumb snatchers around here ain't regular kids like you and the ones where you grew up. These here is niggas and they'll eat somebody like you up. Be taking your lunch money every day."

A look of both sadness and fear covered Secret's face.

"But don't worry. I got you. Hang with me and by the time school starts, you'll be a nigga too."

At the time, Secret wasn't quite sure what being a nigga meant, nor did she care to be one, but what she did want to be was Shawdiece's friend. She liked the foulmouthed girl. Secret had never met anyone like her and found her intriguing. And over time she'd find her to be a good friend who always had her back and would tell her like it is; even though Secret didn't always like what Shawndiece was telling her. Like right now as they sat at the bus stop.

"Just because every other word that comes out of my mouth isn't slang, a curse word, or the N-word, just because I'd rather meet my future husband at a bus stop instead of a club, just because I don't go out with dudes trying to get a tennis bracelet or seven hundred dollar weave doesn't mean I don't know how to handle myself."

Patting her weave while her tennis bracelet gleamed in the sun, Shawndiece said, "So what you trying to say? You trying to lightweight talk about me?"

"I'm just saying," Secret said.

"And you can say it again for all I care. My feelings ain't hurt. It is what it is with you; you know that," Shawndiece said. "Hell yeah, if these muthafuckas wanna shimmer me up, fuck it, I let 'em. They get the pussy, I get the presents. A fair exchange ain't robbery. That doesn't make me a ho. That makes me smart," she reasoned. "These bitches out here giving it up for free, now those the hoes. They spread 'em wide and all they get is a trip to the free clinic. Fuck that shit!"

Secret cast her eyes downward. Shawndiece noticed the somber look on her friend's face.

"Oh, shit," Shawndiece said softly, closing her eyes in regret. She took a deep breath, exhaled, then opened her eyes. "My bad, Secret. That really wasn't supposed to be a shot at you. When I'm trying to hurt you, you know it. My truths do hurt you sometimes and I get that. I do it on purpose because you're the one who used to tell me all the time that the truth will set you free." Shawndiece took her hand and flicked Secret's slicked-back ponytail. "I just want you to be free." Shawdiece's voice almost cracked before she pulled it together. "Hell, one of us gotta get free. Me, I'm a hood rat and I know it. Ratchet and ghetto as fuck!" Shawndiece laughed. Secret didn't.

"No, you're not," Secret said sternly. She went and grabbed Shawndiece by the hands. "I will not allow you to claim that for yourself. You are a bright, beautiful, strong, independent woman. You are a survivor. Shawn, you are my strength," Secret said, looking into her friend's eyes with true sincerity. "Everything you are standing here putting down about yourself is everything I love about you. I love you, girl." Secret released her hands then pointed to Shawdiece's chest. "I love you just how you are. And that's a good thing. So I don't ever want to hear you putting yourself down like that again. Do you hear me?"

All Shawndiece could do was nod. She was both shocked and moved at the moment. She was shocked that Secret called herself getting with her, as she'd always remained soft-spoken. She was moved because no one had ever told her all those positive things about herself.

"Forget that nod. I want to hear you say it. Say, 'I am beautiful and strong.'"

Shawndiece hesitated, but then obliged. "I am beautiful and strong."

"And don't you ever let anybody tell you any different or don't you dare think different yourself."

"Yes, ma'am," Shawndiece said. "Now go on somewhere before you make me cry. And you know I don't cry." Shawndiece looked over Secret's shoulder. "Good; the bus is coming. Now we can stop this hood episode of *Iyanla: Fix My Life*."

Both girls laughed as they retrieved their bus passes. Shawndiece was the first one to step on the bus when it came to a stop in front of them. But before she got all the way up the set of four steep steps she turned around to Secret and said, "You still betta not call that nigga," then proceeded to get on the bus.

Chapter Eight

"So you good?" Lucky asked Major Pain as he entered the lobby after getting checked out at the clinic.

"Yeah, slick dick got a clean bill of health." He grabbed his privates. "We back in business."

Lucky shook his head. "You's a nasty nigga."

"Naw, these bitches out here is the nasty ones. It's them I catch shit from. I ain't catch shit from myself."

"You just don't get it do you?"

"Naw, nigga, you the one who don't get it. That's why you mad at me, 'cause you ain't getting it. Maybe if you got pussy like I gets pussy, yo' ass wouldn't be hating."

Lucky sucked his teeth. "Man, please, don't even front. You see how I do it. I can get any one of these bitches I want."

"Yeah, hood bitches. Anybody can get them. Hell, we done fucked about a dozen of the same bitches. About four of 'em back to back." Major

Pain high-fived Lucky as they walked out of the clinic, heading to the black Cadillac Escalade they rolled in.

"No, that's all you can pull is a hood bitch. I can get real women. Decent women. A chick with a little bit of class about herself and not just a bitch giving up ass to take care of herself and five kids." Five minutes ago Lucky would not have honestly been able to say that, because all the women he'd ever been involved with truly were hood bitches. But for the first time ever, he'd finally met someone different. Secret was definitely not a hood rat. She was of a totally different pedigree.

For a moment, Lucky thought about sharing his encounter with Secret with Major Pain, just to confirm the fact he could pull someone other than a hood chick. He thought better of it though. What if Secret didn't call him back and no real connection was ever made? He'd never hear the end of it from Major Pain. His boy would swear up and down he'd stooped to an all-time new low by having to invent a pretend female. On the other hand, what if she did call him back? What if she was everything any nigga coming up out of the hood could ever want? What if she was wifey material?

When it came to broads, Major Pain was a dirty muthafucka. He'd been known to fuck other people's bitches and not think twice about it. Pussy was this cat's kryptonite. He'd even bedded a few chicks Lucky himself had hit, after the fact. It wasn't like they hadn't shared broads before. It's just that Lucky had been actually diggin' a couple who Major Pain helped himself to without Lucky's consent. Lucky had even toyed with the idea of being with one or two of them on a regular basis. But after finding out they'd smashed the homie, he just couldn't bring himself to do it.

"You shouldn't have told me how good the pussy was," Major Pain had said to Lucky after Lucky called him out on it one time.

Lucky didn't trip. He came to the conclusion that those types of hoes were a dime a dozen. But Secret . . . Naw, Lucky knew she was different, so he'd have to handle her differently. He'd have to protect her from the wiles of the street thugs. So just like her name, he'd keep her his own little secret. Never mind that the exact types of dudes he wanted to protect her from were dudes exactly like himself.

***

Lucky, Major Pain, and their boy Ace were heading out of a nice upscale restaurant located right outside of Flint.

"Good lookin' out, fellas, on the restaurant tip," Ace said as he rubbed his full belly while the three men walked toward the black Escalade they were driving. He'd just been treated to a thick-cut porterhouse, a loaded baked potato, broccoli with cheese, salad, rolls, and glass after glass of wine.

"Aw, homie, you know it ain't nothin' but a thang," Lucky said, giving his partner some dap. "It's the least we could do for one of the best players on the team. Ain't that right, MP?"

"Huh, what?" Major Pain replied, having half been paying attention to the conversation taking place because he'd been so busy texting. The last few words spoken by Lucky eventually registered in his mind. "Oh, yeah. It's the very least." He looked at Lucky and then turned his attention back to his phone.

"You really been holding it down over there on your block," Lucky complimented Ace as he hit the key fob to unlock the SUV.

"I'm just honored y'all even put me on with that spot." Ace climbed in the second row of the three-row vehicle.

Lucky got behind the wheel while Major Pain plopped into the front passenger's seat. "We knew you were the right man for the job," Lucky told Ace.

"That means a lot coming from the head niggas in charge of the game," Ace said. "I mean, it seems just like yesterday I was on the corner trying to prove myself, and now I'm in charge of the most profitable trap in the city. Now I got muthafuckas under me," Ace boasted. "Before you know it, I'ma be like . . ." Ace's words trailed off. It was almost as if he'd had to catch himself from slipping.

"Go on, finish your sentence," Lucky urged Ace. "Before we know it you gon' be like what?" He eyed Ace through the rearview mirror. "Or you just plain ol' gonna be?"

Ace looked puzzled.

"Come on, which is it?" Lucky asked as he drove, his eyes traveling from the road to the rearview mirror to make eye contact with Ace. "Let me guess; before I know it you gonna be like me? Huh, is that it?" Lucky's tone wasn't that of flattery, but that of irritation.

"Well, uh, you know what I'm trying to sa—"

Lucky cut him off. "Or before I know it you are gonna be? Is that what you want, Ace? You're gonna be me." Lucky shot him a look that might not kill, but at least put a nigga in the ICU. "You wanna be me?"

Ace didn't even have a chance to answer. Lucky stopped at a red light and the next thing anyone knew there was a loud bang, a streak of light, and a puff of smoke. Once the smoke had cleared, lying in the back seat with a bullet through his heart was Ace.

His hands were holding his chest where blood spilled between his fingers. His eyes were buck wide and spoke the words, "Am I hit? I can't believe I'm hit. Is this shit for real?"

It only took a few seconds for blood to leak from the corner of Ace's mouth as he inhaled deeply, in one large gulp, but never exhaled.

"Damn shame when a nigga got to take in his last breath," Lucky said as he sat there, the gun still in his hand pointing at his target.

"Yeah, it is kind of fucked up," Major Pain said, taking a moment away from his texting to look at Ace's slumped-over body behind him. "That's what he gets for pinching on our shit and then running his own hustle on the side."

"With our own shit," Lucky added. "Ain't that some shit?"

"Some bullshit." Major Pain shook his head while texting.

"And I really liked dude. For real." Lucky shook his head as well. Lucky turned and looked at Major Pain. "You should have been the one to pull the trigger."

Major Pain stopped texting, looked at Lucky, and asked with a serious mug, "Why?"

"Well, you know what they say," Lucky said with a serious face before both men broke out in laughter when saying in unison, "Don't shoot and drive."

The light turned green and they pulled off, almost oblivious to the bleeding corpse that rested in their second-row seat.

Chapter Nine

Shawndiece watched silently as Secret stared out of the window of the city bus. She could tell her friend had a lot on her mind. Every few seconds or so Secret would exhale, then continue her aimless gaze out of the window.

"What you thinking about? Or do I even need to ask?" Shawndiece said.

Secret just shook her head and exhaled loudly.

"Thinking about what you gonna do? Thinking about whether you're going to go from one clinic to the next?"

Secret shrugged. "Not much to think about. What other choices do I have really?"

"Hell, the same choices our mothers had. But we're here aren't we?"

Secret yanked her attention from the city scene to the girl sitting next to her, who she almost didn't recognize as her friend. "Are you saying what I think you're saying? You? Miss Life Is A Party; Enjoy It? Miss High Spirited Live Life Freely? Be free?"

"And who's to say you still can't do all that? Once again, I refer to our own mothers. Having us didn't stop them from doing whatever they wanted to do in life." Shawndiece sucked her teeth. "And it definitely didn't keep them from running the streets to party."

"Yeah, but I don't want to be that kind of mother. If that's the kind of mother I have to be, then I'd rather not be a mother at all." Secret stared into Shawdiece's eyes.

"Then does that mean what I think it does?"

Secret shrugged again. "Man, Shawn, I just don't know. I don't even want to think about it. I know what I need to do, but then there's the issue of when and how I'm going to do it. I just hadn't thought about all that."

"Then I guess I can give it to ol' dude back at the bus stop."

"What are you talking about?"

"You know the guy from the clinic. At least he kept your mind off the situation. I'll give him that much. Hell, maybe you should call his fine ass after all. Let him be a distraction in your life. He's good on the eyes."

"Oh, so now he's fine?" Secret poked out her lips and rolled her eyes.

"What?" Shawndiece snapped her neck back. "Now I ain't never say dude was ugly or nothing. Just not your type. You can't handle his kind."

Secret shifted her body toward Shawndiece. "Okay, so whose type is he then? Yours? Can you handle him? Is that it? You want him or something?" Secret pulled his number out. "'Cause here, you can have it if it's all like that. He seems to be on your mind way more than he's on mine. So let's nip this in the bud right now." Secret pushed the paper toward Shawndiece. "Here, take it." Secret didn't sound angry, just testy.

"Girl, stop playing." Shawndiece swatted Secret's hand away and Secret stared down at the number. Once again, she exhaled.

Shawndiece stared at Secret for a minute. "Who is he, Secret?" She had the most serious tone yet to her voice.

"I don't know." She put the phone number back away. "I just met him five minutes ago like you did."

"No, I mean who is *he*?" Shawndiece placed her hand on Secret's stomach then whispered, "Who's your baby's father?"

"You don't know him," Secret was quick to say as she cast her eyes downward, then turned back to face the window.

Shawdiece's hand slid from Secret's belly. "Maybe you don't know him. Perhaps that's why you avoid answering the question every time I ask."

Oh, Secret knew who the father was all right, and she didn't need Maury Povich's help in finding out. Ironically, she almost wished she didn't know. Not knowing who her baby daddy was seemed less humiliating and embarrassing than knowing who he was and how he'd come about impregnating her.

Technically, Secret really didn't know him-know him. She knew nothing about him, not even his name. She'd know his face in a lineup if she ever saw him again. Other than that, nothing. She didn't know his favorite color or his favorite food. She knew he liked KFC, but didn't know if it was his favorite. She wouldn't even know the back, dark alley that led to his house, if that was even where he really lived. For all she knew, he could have been using some crackhead's house to get laid while his wife and kids sat waiting for him somewhere in a house in the suburbs.

For that reason alone, she couldn't have the baby that was growing inside her belly; the baby that just a half hour ago back at the clinic she'd learned for certain she was carrying. That had been Secret's whole point in going to the free clinic while Shawndiece tagged along for moral support. Secret's period was two weeks late and she didn't want to wait around with fingers crossed hoping she didn't miss next month's as well. Now, after leaving the clinic, it was official; she was as pregnant as the day was long. And if she dared give birth to this baby, what on God's green earth would she tell the child when it asked who its father was? She would not, under any uncertain terms, give birth to a bastard. She couldn't do that to her child. Poor thing didn't deserve it. No child of hers deserved it.

Besides, she had a plan, a plan to get out of Flint and go make something of herself. How could she do that with a baby in tow? Who would take care of the baby while she went off to college in Ohio? Did they even allow babies in campus dorms? How could she afford a babysitter? She had no money, and how does a mother get child support from a man whose name and address she doesn't even know? Trifling, it was all just trifling. And Secret refused to go out that way. That was not the plan. Then again, it hadn't been in the plan to turn a trick to pay off her estranged father's debt he had with some dangerous guys either, ending up pregnant.

"You know you can tell me if you don't know who you pregnant by don't you?" Shawndiece said, interrupting Secret's secret thoughts. "You know I'm the last person in the world whose gon' judge you. Who am I to judge you about being pregnant when I'm already up on you two abortions? I didn't know whether them babies were Tom's, Dick's, or Khari's." Shawndiece laughed.

"You stupid." Secret chuckled. "Yet here you are telling me to keep mine."

"I'm not telling you to keep yours. I'm just saying I'd understand if you did. Like I said, Secret, you ain't like me. You gon' make it regardless. So if getting an abortion is going to weigh heavy on your mind, you might as well not have all that guilt and remorse holding you back. Hell, you can have sextuplets and you still gon' get further in life than half the chicks in the neighborhood."

"Yeah, but what about college?" Secret reminded her friend. "I've been dreaming of walking the campus of OSU since I can remember. I've looked at their Web site and have sent off for their brochures and I ain't never seen nobody strolling the campus pushing a baby stroller."

"Look, chick, I'm not trying to talk you into anything or out of anything. I just want you to be certain of whatever decision you make. I mean, I can see the pros and cons of keeping the baby and not keeping the baby. It's all about what you want to do. Either way, you know I got your back."

If Secret didn't know anything else for certain, she knew what Shawndiece was saying was true. She'd have her back through hell and high water. She'd never stab her in the back or turn her back on her, but she'd damn sure have her back.

"Now I ain't gonna sit here and lie and tell you I'll babysit for you and all that," Shawndiece continued. "Hell, I ain't wanna have and watch my own babies, so why would I wanna watch yours? But it can call me Auntie Shawn-Shawn and I'll buy it some really cool birthday and Christmas presents."

Secret just looked at Shawn like she was crazy. "Why are you stupid?" She burst out laughing.

"I'm serious."

"I know, and that's the scary part."

The girls continued their ride on the bus until they reached their stop. Once they had gotten off the bus, in their neighborhood, and had walked to the cross streets where they needed to split up, they headed their separate ways.

"Don't forget, I got your back," Shawndiece reminded Secret as she walked in the opposite direction. "And if you decide to go to the next clinic, if need be, I got five on it, you know what I'm saying?"

"Umphf, umphf, umphf. I got no words for you, Shawn, other than I'ma pray for you."

"Good, 'cause I need all the prayer there is." Shawndiece put her thumb to her ear and her pinky finger to her mouth. "Call me," she shouted out as she headed to her house.

"I will," Secret called back as she headed to hers.

Secret could feel her stomach turning as she walked to her house. Her stomach turning had nothing to do with the little embryo, fetus, or whatever it was they call a baby that's barely even a month into development. Her queasy stomach had everything to do with her mother. Whether she kept the baby or not, she'd have to tell her mother. She'd need her either way. The medical card and information came addressed to her mother, and she'd need that card to get some money off the abortion procedure. It wouldn't pay for the full procedure, but it would put a nice little dent in the total cost. She'd learned that when she looked up all her options at the first inkling that she could possibly be pregnant. Nine times out of ten, she'd need her mother to help her pay for the abortion as well. She had just turned eighteen last week, so she didn't need her mother's consent to get the abortion, but she would need her financial support.

She'd thought about picking up a job at the local supermarket real quick. She figured she'd have her first paycheck in enough time before she got too far along in the pregnancy when it would be too late to terminate it. That way she could eliminate having to tell her mother anything at all. But with the whole job application and interview process, she knew she'd be pushing it close. She didn't want to take that chance.

She hated that the thought had even crossed her mind, but just so she could leave her mother out of the whole scenario, she thought about maybe even turning another trick just to get the money she'd need. Her skin crawled at the thought of that, though. She'd made her mind up. She didn't know how, but Secret was going to get rid of that baby so help her God.

Chapter Ten

Secret was so happy when she walked in the door and there was no sign of her mother. She had too much on her mind right now and the last thing she needed was Yolanda nagging and complaining. The last Secret remembered, Yolanda was off work today at her job as a store manager at a local convenience store. She'd either gotten called in or had driven to Detroit to the casino like she was good for doing.

"I hope she hits it big," Secret said to herself as she walked in the kitchen to see what was good to eat. "'Cause I'm gonna need some of that money."

"What did you say? And why you making all that goddamn noise waking me up and shit? I finally get a day off and your ass don't want a bitch to get no rest."

Secret was stunned when she turned around to see her mother's head lifted on the couch. Her mind had been so far gone that she hadn't even seen her lying there on the couch when she walked in the door. As a matter of fact, she couldn't recall seeing her car outside either.

"Oh, I'm sorry, Mom. I didn't even see you lying down there," Secret apologized. "I didn't see your car parked outside either."

"That's because that old bitch a couple doors down let one of her tricks park in my spot again," Yolanda spat. "I had to park way down in the visitor's spot. Next time, whichever nigga she let park in my spot ain't gon' have no money to pay for her pussy because they gon' be too busy replacing all four of their tires. I'ma have that mutherfucker sittin' on bricks fuckin' with my parking spot."

Oh, well, Secret thought as her mother's voice rang loudly in her ears. *Looks like I'm not going to have any peace after all.*

Secret opened the refrigerator and started fumbling through some of the left over containers. The first container she opened was a couple pieces of tilapia her mother had cooked the night before. Secret hated the taste of leftover fish. It just didn't warm up well in the microwave. It turned mushy. The next container was some garlic mashed potatoes that she herself had made. She loved garlic mashed potatoes; the only thing was she couldn't even remember how long ago she'd made them. She made a mental note to clean the refrigerator out before her mother got to cussing and fussing about it. Next she pulled out a container from the back of the fridge. When she opened the lid the sharp smell of old broccoli and cheese assaulted her nose. She quickly put the lid back on it, but the smell lingered.

Secret quickly threw the container back in its spot as she began to gag. She tried to get her throat reflexes under control as she held her stomach. She continued to gag, knowing she'd better make her way to the bathroom and fast.

Like she was trying out for the US track team in the Olympics, Secret closed the fridge door and sprinted to the bathroom. Barely making it to the commode, she quickly lifted the toilet seat and began to heave into the bowl. The smell of the porcelain and that little blue toilet cleaner that hung on the side of the bowl made her puke even more. After about five minutes of heaving and sweating, Secret finally flushed the toilet and pulled herself off her knees. She was startled by her mother standing in the doorway when she turned around to go to the sink.

"You pregnant?" were the distinct, clear, cut-to-the-chase words that came out of Yolanda's mouth.

Still, Secret's reply was, "Huh?"

"What the fuck I tell you about 'huhing' me?" Yolanda said. "Besides, bitch, you heard me." Yolanda walked closer to her daughter. "You knocked up, ain't ya?"

"What makes you say that?" Secret had a stupid look on her face and let out some nervous laughter. Her first instinct was to say, "No, I'm not," but she really didn't want to lie to her mother.

The last time she lied to her mother was when she was in ninth grade. Shawndiece had talked Secret into going to a skip party.

"Your mom has to work today, right?" Shawndiece said to Secret.

"Yes, but—" Secret started before her best friend cut her off.

"Good. That means when the school calls your house to see why you're absent, she won't be there to take the call. If they leave a message, you get home first, so you can just delete it. Miss Yolanda will never know. Come on, girl. You're in high school. Have a little fun for once."

It all sounded easy enough, so instead of getting on the school bus that morning, Secret met up with Shawndiece and they headed over Tico's house, the guy who was hosting the skip party. By the time they got there the party was already jumping. The house was packed with about twenty of the most well-known kids at school. Needless to say, Secret was like a rose in a field of dandelions; she just didn't fit in. Always one to keep her eye on the prize, which was her education, anything outside of school work, homework, and a mall outing here or there with Shawndiece was foreign to Secret. She'd never witnessed this side of high school, and she was in awe.

The other kids were drinking, smoking, and eating the mini-cereal-breakfast buffet Tico had set out. The television was tuned to some BET 106 & Park recordings. It couldn't be heard, though, over the music that was coming out of the living room speakers.

"You cool?" Shawndiece would come over and ask Secret, who'd made permanent residence over in a chair that sat by an end table.

"Yeah, I'm good," Secret would reply, willing herself not to go into her book bag and pull out schoolwork or a book to read. As entertaining as it was to watch the boys and girls at her school who never noticed her—and still weren't paying her a lick of mind—flirt with, touch and grind on each other, she'd prefer to be in class obtaining whatever it would take to get her one day closer to fleeing Flint.

Secret got home that day at the exact same time she would have had she gone to school. Upon walking in the door, she headed straight to the telephone where, just as she'd thought, a message from the school secretary awaited. Secret deleted the message without even listening to it in full, grateful she'd beaten her mother to the message. She'd phoned a couple of her classmates whom she shared most of her classes with and had even been in study groups with before. She managed to get the day's assignments for all her classes and get her work done by the time Yolanda walked through the door that night.

"So how was school today?" Yolanda walked into Secret's room and asked. That alone should have been a red flag for Secret. She couldn't remember the last time her mother had inquired about her and her schooling.

"Uh, it was uh, good," Secret replied, thrown off by her mother's query.

"So what were your assignments today?" Yolanda came and flopped down on Secret's bed.

"Just the same ol' same ol'," Secret said.

"Oh, really? Let's see." Yolanda folded her arms, crossed her legs, and allowed her foot to swing back and forth as if she was calling Secret out, just waiting to bust her in a lie.

Secret pulled out the schoolwork she'd done for the day and handed it to her mother, glad she was able to control her shaking hands.

Yolanda didn't even bother to look it over. She just handed it right back to Secret, glaring at her. "You hungry?"

"Yeah. A little."

"Guess I'll go in the kitchen and whip something up then." Yolanda stood and then headed toward the door.

Secret let out a deep breath. She was in the clear.

"What did you guys have for lunch at school today?" Yolanda turned around and asked. "I don't want to make the same thing you've already eaten." Once again, Yolanda folded her arms. She played the piano on her left arm with her right hand.

"Huh? What?" Secret was stomped.

"I said, what did you all have for lunch at school today?" Now Yolanda's hands were down at her side, balled into fists. Secret stared down at them as if they were talking to her. They were daring her to lie, but begging her not to.

"I don't know." Secret didn't lie. "I didn't eat lunch at school today."

"Why not?"

"Shawndiece and I ate elsewhere." Once again, she didn't lie. She was on a truth roll for sure.

"Where?"

"One of our friend's house." Secret was getting both agitated and nervous. She didn't want to have to lie or, even worse, get caught in one. "Trust me, Ma, you can cook anything and I'll eat it. It's no big deal."

"No big deal, huh?" Yolanda had said in a knowing tone. "Well, since it's no big deal, then I guess I'll leave it alone. But just one more thing."

"Yes, Mom," Secret said, way too eager to get rid of her nagging mother.

"The bus got you to and from school today okay, didn't it?"

Secret's heart was racing. Her mother was being far too inquisitive. *She knows,* Secret thought. *She knows I didn't go to school today.* Secret thought it might be in her best interest to come clean. Then again there was a chance that a simple yes could get rid of her mother and that would be the end of it. With not much time to waste, and before Secret could catch it from slipping through her lips, there was an audible, "Yes."

"And you's a lying motherfucker," were the audible words that shot out of Yolanda's mouth. "Your school called my job looking for yo' black ass. Embarrassed the fuck out of me. I'm sitting there not knowing where my child is. I'm lying telling them you home sick 'cause I don't want them to think I can't keep up with my fast-ass daughter. Where the fuck were you anyway?"

"Nowhere, at school, Ma." Secret wished she could have kicked herself. All she had to do was go ahead and fess up, yet she continued to play along with the lie. That only pissed Yolanda off more.

"So you gon' sit there and lie in my muthafuckin' face like I'm some bitch on the streets?" Yolanda had walked over to the bed where Secret sat and was all up in her face. "Huh, are you?"

"But I was at scho—" Before Secret could even get the lie out, blood was dripping from her lip from the blow Yolanda had struck her with.

"There's two things I can't stand in this world: a thief and a liar," Yolanda told her daughter. "You lie to me, I bust you in your muthafuckin' mouth. Now this is the first time you've ever lied to me that I know of. It happens again, you gon' find yourself on the goddamn floor. When you come to, you gon' feel like someone

88 Treasure Hernandez

*slipped your ass a Mickey 'cause you ain't gon'
remember shit that went down before then. I'm
your mother. You bet' not eva' lie to me or steal
from me. You got that?"*

"Yes, ma'am," Secret said, holding her bleeding lip.

*"Now go take your ass in the bathroom and
clean up for dinner," Yolanda said as she exited
Secret's room, mumbling under her breath,
"You lucky I ain't knock your muthafuckin' teeth
out lying to me."*

*Secret went into the bathroom, her mother's
words ringing in her head.*

"You bet' not eva' lie to me."

"Huh? What?" Secret was startled, her thoughts
from the past returning to the present.

"Didn't I just say don't 'huh' me?" Yolanda
spat as she stood in the bathroom doorway. "Are
you pregnant? And you better not lie to me, girl."

There was no way Secret wanted to hop on the
same merry-go-round she'd ridden her first year
in high school when she decided to tell her first
and only lie to her mother. So this time she just
straight-out told the truth just to get it over with.
"Yes, ma'am, I'm pregnant." She figured now
that she was eighteen, legally an adult, how bad
could it be telling her mother the truth?

Chapter Eleven

The loud, almost obnoxious sound coming from Yolanda's voice box and up her throat ricocheted off the bathroom walls. It took everything in Secret not to just throw her hands over her ears like some four-year-old. She couldn't lie; Secret expected to have to deal with the loudness of her mother's mouth, but what she didn't expect was exactly what was coming out of her mouth.

Laughter.

Wiping the residue of vomit from her mouth with the back of her hand, Secret just stood there looking at her mother like she was crazy. That laugh; it wasn't a happy laugh. To Secret it sounded taunting. She just stood there watching, waiting for the laughter to die down. After what seemed like forever to Secret, it finally did die down.

"Whoooo weeeee!" Yolanda said, holding her stomach. It ached from laughing so hard. "So

Little Miss I'm Better Than Everybody Else, I'm Going to Run Off to College and Make Something of Myself done got herself knocked up?"

Then there it was again, that loud laughter that was agonizing to Secret, not to mention pissing her off now that there were words along with the laughter.

"What I tell you?" Yolanda said, "You just like all the rest of us around these parts." Yolanda raised her hands up and turned full circle until she was facing her daughter again. "You stuck here." She pointed to Secret's stomach. "And whatever you carrying in your stomach is stuck here too. This is the life, sweetheart."

"It wasn't the life for Grandma," Secret was quick to spit. "She didn't live here."

Any smile that had been on Yolanda's face vanished. "Well, you ain't Grandma's daughter. You're your mother's child. The only reason why Mama lived where all those good white folks lived was because she went and married that white man after my daddy was killed."

"Grandpa James wasn't just some white man. He was a good man. A preacher. He's the reason why Grandma found Jesus and got saved. It was God's favor why she went from this ol' raggedy hood life to the good life."

"God favor my ass," Yolanda huffed. "I don't know why you put her on some pedestal. Trust me when I tell you back in the day, your grandma was a force."

Secret was boiling on the inside as her mother spoke ill of the dead. Secret's grandmother had been a lifesaver; there to take them in in their time of need. Perhaps Secret needed to remind her mother of that.

"All I know is that when we lost our house, Grandma was there to take us in," Secret said.

"That's because she'd just found out she'd gotten the cancer," Yolanda replied. "She knew she was going to need somebody there to take care of her with old Grandpa James having already kicked the bucket."

Secret couldn't believe just how cruel her mother could be. She decided she no longer wanted to entertain her mother's negative conversation. So she decided in her grandmother's defense her final words would be, "The grandma I knew was a good woman. She was saved, holy, loving, kind, and was there for us when we needed her. She found Jesus and not only did He save her, but He changed her."

"That's her story and you're stickin' with it too, huh?" Yolanda spat, shaking her head. "That old woman's got you brainwashed, but never mind that dead biddy." Yolanda drew a cross across her heart and looked upward. "God rest her soul." She then focused her attention back on Secret. "What you gon' do now that you got a bun in the oven? You can't stay up in here, that's for sure. The last thing I need is to hear some whiny little baby up at three in the morning looking for its mother's titty. No, ma'am. I ain't the one. But I'm sure you already figured that." She wagged her finger in Secret's direction once again. "So what you gon' do?"

"I hate to bust your bubble, Mama, but my life's plans have not changed one bit," Secret said with more authority than she'd ever used when speaking to her mother. "I'm not proud of my decision, but I have decided not to keep the baby."

"So, what? Is the daddy going to keep it then? He gon' take care of his seed? If that's the case, then I guess you are like Grandma. He must be a white dude, 'cause I know ain't no jive-ass nigga gon' take care of his baby. You watch all those *Behind the Music* and *Unsung* documentaries. Don't nobody but one in five ever got a daddy who raised 'em. That's just niggas for you. So what's his name? What's this little white boy's name who fathered your baby?"

Secret hated how her mother was always seeming to put down their own race. Who did that? For a moment Secret thought her mother just refused to find the good in Blacks, but then she realized Yolanda couldn't seem to find the good in anything or anybody.

"He's not a white boy," Secret said.

"What? A black man willing to raise his own child?" Yolanda put her hands on her slender hips. "Then somebody call *The Guinness Book of World Records* and get this fool inducted immediately." Yolanda began to laugh again.

"Nobody's keeping the baby. I'm getting an abortion!" Secret shouted over Yolanda's laughing.

"What did you say?" Yolanda's tone was indifferent. She really hadn't heard what Secret had said.

Almost cowering down Secret said, "I'm getting an abortion."

Yolanda just stared at her for a few seconds. "Huh, taking the easy way out. Figures." She shook her head.

"Easy? Mama, none of this was easy."

"Oh, but lying on your back and letting some dude crawl up in between your pussy and nut all up in there, giving you a baby, was?"

Secret turned her head in disgust. "Girl, your mama be cracking me up with that mouth of hers. She know she be keepin' it real," Secret could hear Shawndiece saying. In Secret's opinion, if this was keepin' it real—being as vulgar as a porno director—then Secret would take being fake any day.

"Don't act like you disgusted with what I'm saying. If letting some trifling nigga run up in you raw ain't disgusting, then I don't know what is."

"Mama, you act like you didn't let Daddy do the same thing to you," was what Secret wanted to say so badly, but she knew she'd be collecting her teeth up off the floor if she did. So instead, she just stood there boiling inside, biting her tongue.

"Let me stop talking about this poor baby daddy of yours. At least the fool is going to pay for the abortion."

Secret's eyes cast downward.

"He is paying for it isn't he? I mean you the one who got to put your body through all that bullshit. The least he can do is pay for it. I ain't never had one personally, but one of my homegirls did when we were younger and she said it ain't no joke. She said it's like they put a vacuum stick up in you, hit the on button, and just suck the life out of you." Yolanda chuckled. "I guess they are sucking the life out of you." She laughed louder.

Secret cringed.

"Oh, girl, woman up. Put your big-girl panties on. Hell, you done took 'em off to get screwed. Now put 'em back on and go take care of your business. And if you need me to go over the mutherfucker's house with you and get that abortion money, you ain't say nothing but a thang. You might have fucked my daughter, but you ain't about to screw her over."

Secret had to admit, Yolanda's willingness to support her and have her back on trying to shake down the baby daddy for money felt good. Unfortunately, that's not exactly what Secret needed from Yolanda.

"Ma, I'm not trying to do all that," Secret said. She paused before fixing her lips to say, "I was just hoping that, you know, you could help me." Secret swallowed hard. She was nervous about asking her mother anything. Needing help from her mother and actually asking her were two different things. If Secret was lying in the middle of the floor with a knife wound, bleeding all over the place, she felt her mother might help her out of human instinct, subconsciously. But if she straight-out asked her to help her, she felt her mother was the type of person who might let her lie there and suffer a little longer just to spite her—her own natural instinct.

"Help you how?" Yolanda was quick to ask, snapping her neck back.

"Well, I wanted to use the health card to get some money taken off the cost of the procedure. And maybe if I could borrow whatever else I might need, that would be—"

"Hold on." Yolanda put her hand up. "You want me to be the one to take care of you getting an abortion?"

Secret shrugged; then there it was again—that loud, screeching laugh.

"Bitch, you done lost your mind. I wish the fuck I would. All you've done these last few months was walk around here like your shit don't stank, acting like you better than me. And now you want me to help yo' ass. Bitch, fuck you! That's just what you get."

Yes, Secret liked to think she was immune to all the "bitches" and "fuck you's" her mother spewed out. Perhaps it was the pregnancy, but her emotions were on high. It was like with every word that came out of her mother's mouth, her blood began to boil.

Yolanda continued her rant. "Been shitting on me but now you want me to wipe your ass."

Yolanda walked up on Secret and got in her face. "Face it, Mama is always right. This is who you are." She grabbed Secret by the cheeks and turned her head to face the mirror. Both women stared at their reflections. "This is who you are always going to be. You are me."

Words have power. Secret remembered her grandmother telling her that. If her grandmother was accurate, then that meant the words Yolanda had just spoken could possibly manifest themselves. No way Secret could allow that to happen. She'd managed to pretty much remain tightlipped through all of her mother's tirades over the years. But she had to take away the power of her mother's words, even if that meant finally finding a power within herself.

After looking at both her and her mother's reflections, Secret pulled away. "No! I'm not you and you're just mad because you're not me." Secret had been thinking it, but no way had she meant to say it. But the words had slipped out now and there was no taking them back. Secret knew her teeth were as good as gone, so she might as well continue speaking her mind and make it well worth having to wear dentures. "I'm not going to be some project hood rat running around mad at the world. I'm pregnant. I wish I wasn't but I am. If I could turn back the hands of time I would make different decisions, but I can't. This is it."

Secret raised her arms and let them drop back to her side like wet noodles. "But what I am going to do is fix this situation the best I can. Unfortunately that means not bringing another life into this world. But once I'm ready to start a family, with a husband, then that's what I'm going to do. That's part of the plan. But for now, I'm going to take care of the situation; then I'm going to go off to college, as planned, graduate with honors, get a career, start a family, and live happily ever after. The fucking end!" By now tears were streaming down Secret's face. It was a mixture, tears of joy, pain, fear, and relief. It was like she was finally at the end of the rope of mental torture her mother had been strangling her with for so many years. She knew that basically she was grabbing a pair of shears out of her pocket and cutting the rope the same way the doctor had cut her umbilical cord when she was born. Would it be blasphemy to say she felt as if she was being reborn?

"As soon as I get that letter saying I got that scholarship, I'm packing up and I'm gone," Secret continued. "I'm going to become something more than what I could ever be if I stay here. I'm sorry for disrespecting you, Mama, but I'm not you and I'd rather die than become you."

Yolanda had never been more heated in her life. She was having a mental conversation with herself, willing herself not to take her hands and wrap them around Secret's throat until she choked that last breath out of her. She was so mad she began to tremble, reminding Secret of Renee on the *Mob Wives* reality show. Secret coiled back, just waiting for a blow from her mother. A blow was certainly what she got. Only not the kind she'd expected.

"Letter? You mean the letter that came last week addressed to you in care of me? The letter stating you were denied the scholarship?" It was obvious by the look on Yolanda's face that she enjoyed being the bearer of bad news.

Secret, on the other hand, gasped as if the wind had been knocked out of her.

"Yeah, that's right," Yolanda gloated with an I-told-you-so look on her face. "No money, no college. So it looks to me, baby girl, that you ain't got no money for school or an abortion." Yolanda hollered in laughter as she exited the bathroom.

Secret could hear her laughing all the way until Yolanda was behind her closed bedroom door. Even then Secret could hear little chuckles here and there. Still trying to find her breath, and now her strength, Secret held on for dear life to the rim of the sink counter and tried to balance herself. She looked at herself in the mirror. The more she stared at her image, the more it began to transform from her own features to that of her mother's.

"Oh God, no." Secret gasped, managing to go sit down on the toilet lid. She buried her face in her hands. "But I worked so hard." She paused and then looked up. "Why, God, why? I worked so hard to earn that scholarship. Why didn't I get it?"

In a matter of time things for Secret felt as though they'd gone from bad, to worse, to almost unbearable. Not having money for an abortion was one thing, but not having money for college was a whole other animal. "I was just so sure . . ." Secret's words trailed off as her voice began to crack. As far as Secret had been concerned, that full ride to OSU had been in the bag. Even her guidance counselor, who had written a letter of recommendation and submitted the application on her behalf, had been so sure. What happened? Where had things gone wrong?

It looked like Secret had been a moment too short in rebuking the power of her mother's words. Self-pity consumed her, along with devastation, and at this point, she didn't even want to think about college, scholarships, or anything else. She felt like she just wanted to lie down and die.

Secret's stomach began to churn again. This time it was the symptoms of her pregnancy. She looked down at her stomach and wrapped her arms around it. "Poor, baby," she said to her unborn child. "You didn't ask for any of this." She looked around. "Heck, I didn't either."

Secret had been an only child to Yolanda. Her father had three other children: two twin boys and their sister, who was a year older than them. She'd never gotten to know them though. Once the mother of the three children, Rolland's wife at the time, found out about Yolanda, she threatened Rolland to never take her kids around "that woman" . . . "or her child" once Secret was born.

For the most part Rolland had respected his baby mama's wishes. There was one time, though, when he'd taken all four of his children to McDonald's. The two boys roughhoused on the outdoor play equipment while the two girls, glad to have found out they had a sister, talked and played patty-cake-like hand-slapping games.

By the end of the day, the girls felt as though they'd known each other their entire lives. They even cried when it was time for them to part ways. It was like a Nettie and Celie scene from

The Color Purple. Secret was around eight years old at the time and her older sister around ten; it would be the last time they ever saw each other again. Even though Rolland had sworn his four children to secrecy not to tell their mother they'd spent the afternoon with Secret, his oldest daughter couldn't resist. She just had to tell her mother about the sister she always wanted who she now had. The baby mama went off, telling Rolland if he let it happen again she would see him downtown for child support. The words "child support" were any deadbeat dad's kryptonite. Needless to say, Secret never saw her brothers and sister again.

Secret had always felt alone, like there was a void in her life. Perhaps it was the love and nurturing a child can only hope to receive from its mother. Perhaps it was the lack of having a constant father figure and good role model in her life. Maybe it was knowing she had blood brothers and a sister out there who were uprooted from her life before the seed had even been good and planted in the soil. All Secret knew was that she'd longed for that missing piece.

With her hands wrapped around her stomach, that's when it hit Secret. "Maybe you're the missing piece," she mumbled as the light bulb went off in her head.

Secret began to think long and hard about the human life that was growing inside her stomach. No matter how alone Secret might have felt, she knew she wasn't. "As long as I have you, I'll never be alone," she reasoned.

She stood up and walked over to the mirror. "Why can't I keep this baby?" she asked herself. The main reason why she was even considering aborting the baby in the first place was so that she could live her dream of going to college and making a better life for herself. But Yolanda was right: no money no college. She hated to admit it, but as Secret stood in the mirror she wondered if perhaps her mother was right about everything. Secret's destiny appeared to be sewn up in a bag. A life in Flint just like her mother's and every other chick on the block was the life she would live. There was no going up against destiny.

The more Secret thought about things, the more she began to lean toward giving birth versus taking a life. After only a few more minutes, Secret's mind was completely changed and completely made up.

"Oh, well, baby. Looks like it's just going to be you and me," Secret said to her unborn child. But if she was going to keep this baby, she didn't want to be left taking care of it alone.

Her neighborhood was full of single mothers struggling and doing anything and everything they had to do in order to take care of their children. Coming into this world with two parents was hard enough, let alone just one. So Secret decided that since she was going to have the baby, then she'd need to find a father for it. Who would be the lucky guy?

Chapter Twelve

"Lucky? You know you saw me calling you all last night, nigga. Don't try to play me fuckin' stupid."

Half awake, Lucky pulled the cell phone from his ear. Kat's, one of his flavors of the month, blaring voice was not the wake-up call he desired. He looked at the time. It was almost noon. "Damn," he said to himself, mad at himself for sleeping that long.

"Millionaires don't sleep in," he remembered Turf once schooling him.

"Girl, what the hell are you talking about?" Lucky said in a groggy morning voice.

"Yo' tired black ass had me waiting for you at the club all night last night; talkin' 'bout you gon' meet me up in there," Kat roared. "I had my girls all up in there waiting with me, hanging out with me until your ass comes so I wouldn't be up in there by myself. You had me looking like a fool with your no-show ass. And then on top of that you didn't even have the decency to pick up the goddamn phone and call a bitch. You got me all fucked up. You got me mixed up with the next bitch."

Lucky was used to Kat's slick tongue. It got on his nerves, but it was the other things she could do with that tongue of hers that made him keep her around. Any other broad would have gotten told off by Lucky, but he liked Kat. She was cool to have around.

"Damn, my bad," Lucky said in the most genuine voice he could muster up. "I'm sorry, baby. I got caught up in some business."

"Caught up in some pussy is more like it," Kat spat. "I talked to my girl, Taneshia, on the phone last night. She said she'd just seen you at Red Lobster with some ho. What you got to say about that?"

"Man, fuck Taneshia. You gonna listen to that slutty-ass whore? Hell, as quiet as it's kept, that ho wanna fuck me. She'll tell you anything just for me to get on your bad side so she can have a chance at me." Lucky sat up in the bed. "You probably done told her how good this dick is." He grabbed himself and smiled.

"Nigga, please." Kat sucked her teeth. "Don't flatter yourself. What makes you think I be running around bragging about your dick?"

"'Cause it's the best you've ever had. At least that's what you be saying when your ass is riding it." Lucky laughed into the phone receiver.

"That ain't nothing but IATC talk."

"Bitch talk?" Lucky asked.

"No, I said IATC talk. IATC talk. I'm about to cum talk," Kat explained.

"Oh, my fault. I don't speak ho," Lucky joked. But before Kat could snap off on him he said, "Naw, I'm just playing. Baby, you know yours is the only pussy I'm trying to get into. So why don't you bring your fine ass over here and give me some morning pussy?" Lucky looked at the time on his phone again. "I mean some afternoon pussy?"

Kat sighed. Lucky assumed that in the brief moment of silence, she was pondering whether to accept his invitation.

"Girl, come on. You know you want to come over here and get some of this lucky dick."

"Ohhhh, I hate you. You are so full of yourself."

"Naw, you hate yourself, 'cause you know I'm right. And you want to be full of me. So quit wasting your cell phone minutes on that cheep-ass phone of yours and get over here."

Kat paused before saying, "Give me about thirty minutes," then hung up the phone.

Lucky pulled the phone away from his ear, looked at it, and smiled while shaking his head. He didn't know whether he was just smooth like that, or if hood rats were just vulnerable like that.

"What did she say?"

Lucky looked over at Taneshia, one of Kat's best friends, who was lying beside him buck-naked. "She'll be here in a half hour, so you better hurry up, take a shower, and get to moving." Lucky sat up, fixing to get out of the bed.

"Whoa, whoa, wait up, baby," Taneshia purred as she pulled Lucky back by the arm. "Where you going? You gon' just wake up and leave all this right here?" Taneshia pulled the cover back to display her dark chocolate body.

Lucky looked at her. Somewhere within that chocolate bush of hers, something was calling his name to come closer. "Damn, baby, your shit is beautiful. It's like a manicured lawn or some shit." Lucky dang near foamed at the mouth. Next, his eyes roamed to her breasts. She had the biggest, darkest nipples he'd ever seen in his life. He became hypnotized by them. The longer he stared at them, the more he yearned for them like a baby would its mother's breast during feeding time.

As Lucky slid back into the bed, one hand went straight to rubbing Taneshia's privates as his other hand gripped one of her breasts. He took the large nipple and shoved it into his mouth. It filled his mouth up like one of those extra-large Blow Pops. He sucked and slurped like different flavors of Kool-Aid were coming out.

"Ummm," Taneshia moaned as she placed one of her hands on top of Lucky's hand that was on her crotch. She began to guide his hand over her lawn. "I love when you touch it."

"You like that, huh?" Before Taneshia could answer, Lucky thrust his tongue into her mouth while simultaneously thrusting his middle finger inside her.

"Uhhhh," Taneshia moaned in ecstasy as she began squirming her hips while locking her walls tightly around Lucky's fingers.

"That's right; rock wit' it, baby," Lucky whispered. He pulled his head back. He watched Taneshia, with her eyes closed, twist and groan to his touch as he fondled her breast, plunged his middle finger inside of her while massaging her clit with his thumb. Talk about multitasking. "You wet as fuck," Lucky said, his dick as hard as rock as he got turned on by both the sound and the touch of Taneshia's wetness.

After taking her out on a dinner date to Red Lobster last night, he knew she was going to repay him with some off-the-chain, mind-blowing sex. And she had, right in the back seat of his truck in the restaurant parking lot. All the while his phone was blowing up. He knew it was Kat because he'd promised to meet her out at one of the clubs. He was already an hour late at the time, but no way was he coming up out of Taneshia's pussy. As far as he was concerned, a bird in the hand was worth two in the bush . . . and damn did Taneshia have a bush!

"I know we already had dinner and it's kind of backward," Taneshia had told Lucky last night after they had both climaxed and were sitting in his truck getting their clothing back in order. "But if we go to your place, I'll give you a tossed salad."

At first Lucky was a little thrown by Taneshia's comment until he remembered Chris Rock's old standup show in which he referred to anal sex as tossing a salad. Lucky's dick got hard all over again. Before he could reply, Taneshia's cell phone had rung.

"While you think about it, let me take this call," Taneshia had said, then hit the TALK button on her phone. "Hello." She looked dead into Lucky's eyes while saying, "Hey, Kat."

Lucky watched to see how Taneshia would handle herself on the call with Kat, knowing she'd just finished fucking her man.

"For real? He stood you up again? That explains why I just saw him at Red Lobster with some ho," Taneshia said, smirking at Lucky. "Girl, you know I wouldn't lie to you. Yes. I'm sure it was him. No, I didn't recognize her from around the way. You know I'm already on probation for that fight I got into with my auntie. I wasn't trying to get with her and have the police called and shit, or else you know I would have had your back under any other circumstance. All right, girl. You take care." Taneshia was about to end the call before she said, "Oh, yeah, we still going to get our nails done tomorrow? Cool, I'll get at you tomorrow then. Bye, girl."

Lucky watched in amazement as Taneshia ended the call, turned to him, and said, "Nigga, what? You meeting up with her or you taking me back to your place to do things to me that lame bitch would never allow?"

No words needed to be spoken as Lucky put the pedal to the metal. The choice had been made. Now here he was the next morning going for seconds.

"Ooooh, Lucky," Taneshia whined, pumping her hips up and down in the air. "Stick it in."

Lucky removed his finger from Taneshia and placed his wet finger to her lips. She sucked her own juices off of it. He reached over behind his back and tried to blindly grab a condom from his nightstand. He fiddled around until gripping a string of three. He placed the top of the strand between his teeth and tugged, leaving the lone condom pack in his mouth. He threw the other two over his shoulder. With the condom packet still between his teeth, he used his hand to rip it open. He spit out the piece of packaging that remained in his mouth while pulling the condom out of the opened package. He slipped on the condom and then slipped into Taneshia. He slid into her like a baseball player slides into home base.

"Goddamn this shit is wet," he said, dipping in and out of her.

Taneshia lay flat with her legs opened frog style. Her legs bounced in the air with every plunge Lucky made inside her. His lower half lay flat between her legs while his arms held his upper body up. After a couple more in-and-out plunges, he began to dig deep in her in a motion as if he was climbing a wall.

"Oh, shit," Taneshia growled between her teeth. "You hittin' that spot right."

"That's the spot?" Lucky reconfirmed as he continued his climb.

"Hell, yeah. Hell yeah, motherfucker." Taneshia began to throw her hips back at Lucky, making her legs bounce even harder.

"Damn, you gon' make me cum. Bitch, you 'bout to make me . . . cummmmm!" Lucky said as he filled the condom up with his sticky, icky fluids.

Taneshia, realizing Lucky was cumming but she hadn't yet, quickly pushed Lucky to the side, pulled the condom off, and began playing with herself with Lucky's wet, but still hard, dick.

"That's right, get yours, fuck it, baby," Lucky cheered her on.

"Oooohhhh, ooooohhhh," Taneshia moaned as she straddled Lucky, smacking his dick up against her clit.

"That's right; get that dick, baby," Lucky said as he watched Taneshia's mouth open and he let out a long moan.

Taneshia began to tremble. "I'm cummin'. I'm cummin'. Oh God." After a couple more flicks of his dick onto her clit, Taneshia pressed his manhood against her clit, exhaled, and then fell onto his chest.

The two lay there with their chests heaving up and down. A couple minutes later there was a knock on the door.

"Oh, shit, that's Kat," Taneshia said, rising up and looking at the bedroom doorway. "What are we going to do?"

Lucky, fully satisfied and worn out, looked to Taneshia and said. "Let the bitch knock; that's what we're going to do."

Taneshia giggled, pulled the covers over both her and Lucky, then slid under the covers to put her mouth on him. She sucked and slurped while Kat knocked and knocked.

Chapter Thirteen

"Oh, shit, damn, girl," Lucky said as he clutched Taneshia's hair while ejaculating in her mouth.

"Mmmm." Taneshia came up from under the covers while wiping her mouth. Even with all of Kat's pounding and knocking at the door, she was able to keep a good rhythm while bobbing her head. Halfway through giving Lucky a blow job, Kat's knocking had stopped, but the ringing of Lucky's phone started. The couple knew it was Kat calling to curse Lucky out good.

The phone hadn't rung in about five minutes. Lucky figured Kat had grown tired of her useless efforts to contact him. No sooner than that thought crossed his mind, the phone started ringing again.

"Damn, I might as well answer the phone," Lucky reasoned. "This bitch gon' blow me up until she gets shit off her chest and cusses me out."

"Well, I'm gonna go take a shower and get cleaned up," Taneshia said, getting out of the bed, gathering her clothing, and heading into the bathroom.

"Yo," Lucky said into the phone, without even looking at the caller ID. He simply prepared himself for the wrath of Kat.

As far as Lucky was concerned, this was his and Kat's weekly ritual. He'd do something to piss her off. She'd get pissed off. She'd cuss him out to the tenth degree, calling him everything under the sun but a child of God. He'd let her get that off then promise to make it better. He'd either make it better or fuck up again. This time he'd fucked up again. Either way, he knew Kat wasn't going anywhere. He'd been hitting that on and off since she was fourteen. Lucky had been her first, so he knew he had that type of hold on her. Besides, Kat was a hood chick, a bottom bitch. She knew her role. She may not have liked her role, but she knew it. So either she played the role she was given, or she bowed off the stage gracefully and let another chick be the leading lady.

"I'm in the streets," Lucky would always tell her. "I'm a street nigga and you know how this life is. Ain't no rules. Ain't no schedules and agendas. Ain't no promises and commitments.

This life is what it is. You either ride and die or find you a nine-to-five cat."

That was the ultimatum Kat accepted, but even though she accepted it, that didn't stop her from putting up a fight. She knew Lucky couldn't live this life forever. And once he got too old for the streets and had to pass the reins and go settle down somewhere like the predecessors before him, she'd be right there waiting. She often referred to herself as one of those white-girl NBA chicks. They let a nigga do whatever and whenever, just as long as he wifed them once he got that big-ass contract. Kat was going to be there for Lucky, and not just for the money the life he lived granted him, but because she really did have a soft spot in her heart for Lucky. Of course, she'd never let him know that. That would have him running all over her all the more. But she always made sure she put up just enough fight to let him know when the time did come for him to wife her, she wasn't going to take all his shit.

"Yo," Lucky repeated again into the phone receiver.

"Lucky? Is that you?"

He didn't recognize the soft, sweet, subtle voice he heard coming through the phone receiver. Lucky sat up in the bed with a confused look on his face.

"Yeah, this is me. Who dis?"

There was a matching soft, sweet, subtle chuckle now intoxicating Lucky's ear.

"Who is this?" He really wanted to know. He pulled the phone away from his ear to check the caller ID. The word restricted was on his screen.

"That's more like it; 'who is this' versus 'who dis.'"

"Well . . . who is it?"

"Hmmmmm. How about I give you a hint?"

Lucky imagined the owner of the voice licking lips that were smothered in pink glittery lip gloss.

"But just one. And if you don't guess, I'm going to hang up and you'll go to your grave never ever knowing who the girl behind the mysterious voice was who called your phone one Saturday afternoon in June."

"Damn, it's like that?"

"Just like that," the voice cooed.

"All right then, give me a hint."

"Okay, let me think for a minute." There was a few seconds of silence before the "shhhhhhh" sound came through the phone.

"Shhhhhhhhh?" Lucky repeated. "That's my hint?"

"Yep. That's your hint."

"That ain't no hint. I thought you were trying to tell me to be quiet so you could tell me the hint or a secret or something." No sooner than Lucky got the last sentence out of his mouth it hit him like lightning in the worst thunderstorm ever. "Secret?" Lucky let it slip out of his mouth. "Secret, is this you?"

"If I tell you, will you keep me all to yourself . . . just like a secret?"

"You are one secret definitely worth keeping to myself." Subconsciously, Lucky had a mile-long smile on his face that just wouldn't go away.

"I like that," Secret said, busting out laughing, breaking character.

"I take it this is you? What's up, mama?" Lucky slid down a little, getting comfortable in his bed. "I'm glad you called. Now I can get rid of all these pins and needles I've been waiting on for the last forty-eight hours."

"What? You mean to tell me it's only been two days since I met you? Dang," Secret said with disappointment.

"Why, what's wrong?"

"My girl had told me to make sure I waited at least a week to call you so that I wouldn't seem desperate. I guess these past two days in wait have felt like a week."

Lucky let out a cocky laugh as his ego grew. He knew when somebody was fucking with his head in order to blow him up. He'd frequented enough strip clubs to know the shit-talking game females put on a nigga. Still, he liked it. It was different coming from Secret. She was different.

"You know I'm just messing with you, right?" Secret said.

"Yeah, but sometimes a nigga need to be messed with."

"As it is for a woman," Secret replied.

"Yeah, but I'm sure you got dudes all over the place trying to win your heart," Lucky fished. He had a sense that wasn't the case with Secret, but still he wanted confirmation from her own mouth.

"Actually, I don't. Honestly, men haven't been my focus. I was wrapped up in doing something the women in my family rarely did, which was graduate high school. And I did so with honors."

"High school? How old are you? You are legal ain't you? I ain't trying to go out like Romeo."

Secret knew Lucky was referring to the character Romeo from *The Steve Harvey Show* sitcom who'd been gunned down as a result of some underage female he'd had sex with. "Yes, I'm legal. Eighteen. How old are you?"

"I'm legal too. Let's just put it that way," Lucky replied.

"And I thought it was a woman who never wanted to tell her age. You must be an old man. I'm not going to need to have you a walker waiting when we go out on dates am I?"

"Oh, so you're going out on a date with me, huh?"

Secret chuckled. "Dang, once again, I don't think my girl would approve of my moving so fast."

"I like it fast. I like my shit now." Fearing he'd sound too eager, give Secret the wrong idea, or just scare her away period, Lucky pulled the reins back some. "But we can take things slow if that's how you like it."

"Mmmm, yeah. I like it slow, Lucky."

Lucky pulled the phone away from his ear, looked at it, and whispered to himself, "Goddamn." He liked how this girl was talking. He put the phone back to his ear. "Then slow it is." Just then he heard the shower water turn off. He knew within minutes Taneshia would be making her way out of the bathroom. He decided to hurry along his conversation with Secret. "So what about that date? Do you think a brotha could pick you up sometime and kick it with you?"

"That sounds good."

"So when's a good time for you? The weekend, the weekdays?"

"Well, school is out and I'm really not working right now, so I can go around your schedule."

"Well, high school days are well behind me and I'm . . ." Lucky paused and thought for a minute. "I guess I'm what you would call an entrepreneur."

"Oh, yeah, well what is it exactly that you do?"

"I do enough and make enough so that when I come pick you up for our date, you can go anywhere and get anything you'd like. So like I said, you name the time and place and let's make it happen."

Secret set up a date to see Lucky in two days at eight p.m. She then gave Lucky the address for him to pick her up at.

"I got a feeling the next forty-eight hours is going to feel like a week," Lucky said. "But I'll get through it."

"I'm sure you will," Secret replied. "Well, I guess I'll let you go. I look forward to seeing you, Lucky."

"Same here," Lucky replied and then ended the call. It was perfect timing, too, because just as soon as he hung up with Secret, Taneshia came out of the bathroom fully dressed, towel drying her wet and curly weave.

"So what did she say?" Taneshia asked Lucky.

"Huh?" he questioned, his thoughts being pulled away from the conversation he'd just had with Secret.

"What did Kat's crazy ass say?"

"Oh, that?" He looked at the phone. He then looked back up at Taneshia and said, "It's a secret."

"Bitch, I feel like we on some Disney or Nickelodeon show where I'm feeding the nerd the lines she needs to speak to her hot date," Shawndiece said as she snatched her cell phone from Secret's hands.

Secret couldn't help but sit there and chuckle as she fell back onto Shawdiece's bed.

"And you think this shit is funny? What the hell you gonna say when you face to face with dude and I ain't there to feed your ass no fly-ass lines? Let me see how funny you think the shit is then."

"Oh, girl, stop tripping." Secret sat up and hit Shawndiece on the arm. "That was cute and you know it. And I must say, you got some slick little lines. No wonder you be getting tennis bracelets and cell phones and stuff."

"Um, hmmm. Now maybe you can get that nigga to buy you a cell phone so you won't have to use mine to call his ass."

"What do I need a cell phone for? You're the only friend I have and you live five minutes away."

"Yeah, well, it just ain't normal for a teenager not to have a cell phone. An iPod, something . . . if just for GP, general purpose, damn!"

"Well, I have bigger issues and needs than just some stupid cell phone." Secret took on a serious tone.

Empathizing with the dilemma her best friend was facing, Shawndiece went and put her arm around Secret's shoulders. "Don't worry, mama. You got this. Everything is going to work out just fine."

Secret stood up and walked over to Shawdiece's bedroom window. "I don't know. I don't feel right about all this. Lucky seems like a cool guy." She turned to Shawndiece. "I feel like I'm maybe tricking him or something."

"There is no maybe about it. Ho, you are tricking him." Shawndiece began to laugh. After a few seconds she realized that Secret did not think her comment was so funny. "Look, chick. You knocked up. You want the baby but you want some help raising it. You act like the real father is Big Poppa from *Real Housewives of Atlanta* and don't want nobody to know."

"It's not like that," Secret interrupted.

"Well, whatever it's like, we've got a situation. And if you ask me, we now have a resolution." Shawndiece spoke sternly and direct. "You hook up with Lucky. Spend every moment you can with him like you're in some whirlwind fantasy romance. Give up the nookie. A couple weeks later take a pregnancy test and let that nigga know he 'bout to be a daddy. Bitches do it all the time. Don't lose no sleep. That shit is just another Tuesday in the hood."

Secret looked at Shawndiece and shook her head. "You act like this is normal. I mean, Shawn, this isn't just a little lie that I can eventually sweep up under the rug. I'm going to have to live and keep up with this one for the rest of my life." It was clear Secret was having second thoughts. "I just don't know if I can go through with this."

"Secret, do you know how many dudes are out there taking care of the product of another man's nut? The mama ain't stuttin' his ass knowing he probably done had God knows how many kids on her that she don't know about it. He taking care of other bitches' kids so he might as well take care of another nigga's."

"You are so cold," Secret said, stifling a laugh, not because she thought it was funny to play people like that. She thought it was funny how her best friend seemed to think it really was normal.

"Like I said; it's business as usual in the hood. Shit that's normal in the hood may not be the normal for society outside of our world. Just think, if it wasn't for rap music, people would still be clueless as to some of the shit that really goes on in the hood." Shawndiece stated. "But you can look at it this way, too: let the lie be short-lived by going ahead and getting an abortion. Go ahead and hook up with this Lucky nigga and all that other stuff. But just when you tell him that you are pregnant, let him know you want to get an abortion. He'll pay for it." Shawndiece wiped her hands clean. "Either way it goes, issue resolved."

Secret rubbed her belly. "But I don't want an abortion. Not now. What's the use? This is my life. This is what it is. This is what it's meant to be. No need trying to fight it. It's ordained. If it ain't this baby it's going to be another one."

Shawndiece hated the look of defeat she saw in her friend. She wasn't used to that coming from Secret. Secret had always had a plan for her life and had been hell-bent on sticking to it. That plan was going to take her away from Flint where she'd live a prosperous and successful life. She no longer saw that fight and determination in Secret anymore.

"A baby is not the end of the world, Secret," Shawndiece told Secret as she pushed her friend's bangs back from her forehead. "You can still live your dream."

"Look, forget about dreams. This is the real world. This is my reality," Secret said with conviction. "Now let's head down to your kitchen so you can do my hair. I got a date with my baby daddy coming up."

Inside, Shawdiece was a little saddened that her efforts to talk Secret into sticking to her dreams fell on deaf ears. She really wanted Secret to be the one to succeed in life. But it was clear Secret's mind was made up. And as promised, Shawdiece would have her best friend's back no matter what. "Yeah, plus I need to school you a little more on how you need to play the type of nigga like Lucky."

Shawndiece smiled, then led the way to her kitchen, where she would begin the process of transforming Secret from a book-smart good girl to a streetwise hood girl.

Chapter Fourteen

"You sure this skirt isn't too short?" Secret looked down at the denim mini skirt she was wearing compliments of Shawndiece. "And this shirt makes my boobs look extra big."

"Girl, it ain't the shirt; it's that good bra you wearing," Shawndiece told her.

The two were standing in front of the full-length mirror on the back of Shawdiece's bedroom door. Secret had decided to have Lucky pick her up at Shawdiece's house to avoid any chances of Lucky encountering her mother. The last thing Secret needed was for her mother to bring up the fact that she was pregnant and ruin the entire plan.

"Skylar bought it for me from Victoria's Secret." Shawndiece cupped her hands underneath Secret's breasts and adjusted them. "It's expensive, so make sure you take care of it. Don't get into any of that wild sex where niggas

start yanking your panties and bras off thinking
that shit is sexy, all the while you want to send
they ass a bill to replace yo' shit."

Secret laughed. "Well, I wouldn't know anything about all that, and it doesn't sound like
something I want to know about." She smacked
Shawdiece's hands away. "Now stop molesting
my boobs and fix this piece of hair that won't
stay."

Shawndiece worked part time at the hair
salon her mother owned, but she did more heads
out of her kitchen. She still had to earn several
more hours in order to earn her certificate from
the School of Cosmetology. If the state was to
come in and bust her at her mom's salon, the
whole shop could get shut down. She didn't want
to put her mother in jeopardy any more than
she had to. But when her clients wanted services
that were better suited to be done in the shop,
Shawndiece did that at her mother's shop.

"I'm going to be hair stylist to the stars some
day," Shawndiece would say more so in play
mode versus something she really believed could
happen for her.

"If you hadn't changed shirts a million
times, then a hair wouldn't be out of place."
Shawndiece grabbed the rat's tail comb that sat

on her dresser and began to use the end to tuck any loose strands of hair from Secret's up-do.

"You sure that black one doesn't go better with this skirt than this orange one?" Secret tugged at the shirt she was wearing. To her, it was showing far more cleavage than she was used to. As a matter of fact, she wasn't used to showing any cleavage at all. So she surmised that perhaps it was okay.

"We not even 'bout to go there again," Shawndiece spat, smacking the comb back down on the dresser. She was fed up with Secret second-guessing her outfit choices numerous times. "You wearing that shirt." She looked her up and down. "You wearing that skirt and you wearing those wedges."

Just then the doorbell rang.

"Perfect," Shawndiece said. "Now you don't have time to change anything even if you wanted to. Now grab that orange Michael Kors bag and let's go."

Secret, feeling like she was Shawdiece's little Barbie doll about to go on her first date with Ken, grabbed the purse, again compliments of Shawndiece. She strutted in the wedges she'd practiced wearing for about a half hour over to the bedroom door where Shawndiece stood waiting for her. She was excited to be going on her first date, regardless of her underlying intentions. On the flip side, she felt a little guilty inside as well. But every time guilt reared its ugly head she'd remind herself that she was doing this for the baby.

"Whoooo weeeee. Look at you lookin' like Beyoncé." She put her hand on Secret's belly. "Don't worry, Blue Ivy, we gon' find you a daddy Jay-Z."

"Will you stop it with your crazy self?" Secret said, slapping Shawdiece's hand off of her stomach.

"'Got me lookin' crazy,'" Shawndiece began her own personal rendition of Beyoncé and Jay-Z's hit collaboration. She could tell she was starting to aggravate Secret as Secret rolled her eyes at Shawdiece. "Okay. Okay, I'm sorry. Let's go."

The two headed down the steps just as the doorbell rang again. When they hit the bottom landing of the steps they each stopped and just stood there.

"What?" Shawndiece asked Secret.

"Aren't you going to answer the door?" Secret asked.

"Aren't you?"

"It's your house."

"It's your baby daddy," Shawndiece countered.

"Girl, get the damn door." Secret pushed Shawndiece toward the door.

"If you can't open the door for him, how you gon' open your legs?" Shawndiece mumbled under her breath as she opened the door. "Well damn! Maybe I should have given your ass my number." Shawdiece's hand flew over her mouth. "Did I just say that out loud?"

"Uhhh, yes, you did," Secret came up behind her and said, placing her hand on Shawdiece's shoulder and pulling her out of the way.

"See? I told you to get the door," she whispered.

Secret just rolled her eyes up in her head and looked to Lucky, who was standing there with a smile on his face, looking as dapper as could be.

"Sorry about my rude friend," Secret told him. "But I can't say I blame her for the Freudian slip."

"Oh, it's all good," Lucky said. He stood there dressed in his Sean John button-up shirt with Sean Jean jeans. His blue, white, and gray Nikes matched the blue, white, and gray plaid pattern on his shirt. His eyes looked mysterious under the brim of his blue snap-back Nike hat, and his goatee was razor sharp.

"You look nice," Secret complimented. *This is for the baby.* She had to remind herself of this as she felt guilt rising again.

"So do you." He gave her the once-over. "Lookin' like an around-the-way girl," he joked. What had attracted Lucky to Secret was that she was different from all the rest of the girls, but now here she stood greeting him at the door dressed like all the rest. He hoped he wasn't being duped.

"You have me to thank for the look Miss Secret is wearing tonight," Shawndiece jumped in. "I styled her and am willing to style for the stars. Just send them my way." Shawndiece brushed invisible dirt off her shoulders.

Lucky looked to Secret for confirmation.

"Yes, I have to give Shawndiece credit for this getup," Secret admitted, her tone letting Lucky know this wasn't her typical style.

His guard went down. This explanation took care of his concerns. "Now all you need to be doing is waiting at the bus stop sucking on a lollipop."

Secret laughed with him at the reference to the throwback LL Cool J song. "Well, I've already done the bus stop part, remember?"

"All right, you two, enough of the pleasantries. I've got a date too," Shawndiece spoke up. She looked to Lucky. "You don't mind dropping me off around the corner right quick before you head out to wherever you going do you?"

Now Lucky looked Shawndiece up and down in her dark denim skinny jeans, green T-shirt, and green patent leather stilettos. She toted a green leather Ralph Lauren bag. "So you got all cleaned up for a brotha and he can't even come pick you up at your doorstep? You gotta go meet him out," he said to Shawndiece.

"Oh, not by his choice," Shawndiece clarified. "He got wheels; it's just that you can't let everybody know where you live at. I'ma meet him out, read him, and see how things is. If he all weird or something or have stalker characteristics, I'm probably gon' text Secret to have y'all scoop me up on y'all's way back home. Is that cool?" Shawndiece was as serious as a law school hopeful about to take their LSAT exam.

"Well, damn, seeming you have this whole thing planned out, I wouldn't want to ruin your plans and all, so I guess it is cool." Lucky chuckled. "What the hell, you just wanna go out on our date with us and just say fuck ol' dude all together?" He was being sarcastic.

"Naw, but good lookin' out," Shawndiece said as she dug her keys out of her purse and turned out the lights. That was everyone's cue to head out of the house.

Lucky extended his hand to aid Secret in stepping out of the house and onto the porch. "Your hands are so soft," Lucky told her.

"Thank you," Secret said. She hoped the makeup Shawndiece had put on her was hiding all the natural blushing of her cheeks.

Shawndiece locked the door and then followed Lucky and Secret to his SUV.

"Dang, this is you, Lucky?" Shawndiece said while ogling the beautiful, shining rims on his fully loaded Escalade. "You sho' is lucky. I likes this."

"Thanks, ma," he said as he clicked open the locks and proceeded to open the door for Secret. "Hold up, I got you, too," he said to Shawndiece once he saw her about to get inside the backseat of the truck. "Damn, what kind of cats do you be dating for real? You ain't used to waiting for a dude to open the door for you?"

Shawndiece blushed and remained silent. Her answer would be in the negative. The only things most dudes were quick to open for her was a condom.

Both Secret and Shawndiece eyed each other, impressed by the chivalry Lucky was displaying.

Once Lucky got Secret all comfy inside the vehicle, he did the same for Shawndiece and then walked around to the driver's side and got in. "I'm heading up north. Where you want me to drop you off?" Lucky asked Shawndiece before pulling off.

"Just drive. I'll let you know," Shawndiece replied as they pulled off from in front of her house. After driving about a half mile Shawndiece pointed out a house. "Right here. This is good. The yellow house right there." She continued pointing.

Lucky pulled up to a house that had several people hanging out on the front porch, shooting the breeze. Shawndiece went to open the door to get out.

"Girl, will you just hold up? I said I got you, dang," Lucky said.

"Oh, yeah, my bad," Shawndiece said as Lucky got out of the car. She then quickly leaned into Secret's ear. "Girl, it's all good. Ain't no other niggas tucked nowhere in the truck or anything, so you good to go."

Shawndiece had insisted on pretending that she needed a ride from Lucky just so she could scope out the truck and make sure Lucky didn't have any of his boys inside pretending like they needed to be dropped off somewhere.

"Girl, you fresh meat and a dog can smell fresh meat a mile away," Shawndiece had warned Secret. "And no matter the dog, they always got tricks. That nigga been done got you up in his car, have all his boys waiting inside thinking they gon' get a piece of you too. That's what happened to Tashayda. They slipped something in her drink and she for real-for real don't know who the daddy of her baby is."

Shawdiece's cautionary tale had convinced Secret to go along with the little charade of her needing a ride to meet her date; all the while she was really just going over her cousin's house to kick it. And of course, there was no way she'd planned on texting Secret to come pick her back up considering Secret didn't have a cell phone. That was just another tactic to let Lucky know she'd be checking in on her girl, so not to do anything stupid.

"Thanks for everything," Secret told Shawndiece as Lucky opened her door for her.

"Have fun." Shawndiece kissed Secret on the cheek and then hopped out of the car.

Shawndiece headed up the steps where she was greeted by all the people on the porch with high fives, hugs, and "what up's."

"So you ready to ride?" Lucky asked Secret as he parked himself back in the driver's seat and closed the door.

"Yep, all ready," Secret lied. She was far from ready. She was as nervous as all get-out. She really wanted for him to let her out of the car so she could run and get some last minute advice from Shawndiece. But it was too late. Lucky pulled off. Now she was all on her own.

Chapter Fifteen

"Wow! This place is soooooo cute," Secret said as she stepped into the dining area. When they'd first pulled up to what looked like a house, a big house, almost mansion-like, she was a little skeptical. Shawndiece had pounded it in her head that she was only to go to a public place with him. No stopping off over one of his boys' house so he could pick up something; none of that okey-doke. Shawndiece had warned her and given her scenarios to so much bad stuff that could happen.

"It's this li'l bed and breakfast–type spot I stumbled on once upon a time," Lucky had told Secret, which had relaxed her and enabled her to allow Lucky to escort her from the car into the facility.

Secret found the décor to be exquisite.

"Yeah, I figured you'd like it," Lucky said, all but patting himself on the back. "It takes a special kind of girl to appreciate this type of thing." He looked around, admiring the not-too-fancy, but classy décor. The room could seat about twenty parties. It had a high ceiling with a chandelier hanging over each table that one might find in a middle-class home dining room. The tables were draped in white linen. The tables alternated with having a candle as a centerpiece or a flower in a crystal vase. The chairs were high back with a white cushion seat. The floors were hardwood, but each table was set upon a round white and gold rug that from a distance made it look as though each table was floating on a lily pad in a pond. It was darling and sophisticated; something Lucky figured a regular hood chick would think was corny and whack. He figured they'd prefer some expensive steak and lobster joint with a crowd for them to be seen.

"So, I'm special?" Secret asked.

"Huh," Lucky stammered.

"You said it takes a special kind of girl to appreciate this type of thing. So does that mean I'm special?" Secret stood there with her hands clasped in front of her, blushing and looking pure and innocent.

"Girl, you know you're special," Lucky answered. "You don't need me to tell you that. You're not like any of the other girls from these parts. As a matter of fact, are you from here?"

Before Secret could answer, a little blond-haired white woman, who appeared to be around her mid-forties, approached the couple. "Ahhhh, you must be our Lucky couple," the woman greeted.

"Yep, that's us, the Lucky couple," Lucky replied.

"I thought it was just way too cute when our receptionist told us someone had called and reserved the entire dining room for tonight for just two people. And when I asked her the lucky couple's name, she replied, 'Lucky.'" The woman was cracking herself up as she held her stomach with laughter. "'What a lucky couple,' I told her . . . no pun intended." The woman lightly elbowed Lucky on the arm and bent over laughing.

Secret looked at Lucky and couldn't help but be amused by the woman's antics.

"Ahhh, anyway," the woman said, getting herself together. "I'm Brook, part owner. My partner, Casey, who happens to be my re-al-life partner, and I have been running this place for the past three years now. We'd like to say it's one of Michigan's best kept secrets."

"I've never heard of it," Secret admitted, "but it is indeed a beautiful place you have here."

"Well, thank you. But tonight, this place belongs to you. Just you. Now let me show you to your table." Brook escorted Lucky and Secret to a table that was smack in the center of the room that donned a flower in a vase as its centerpiece. "My cousin Dustin, who is your own personal chef, will be out momentarily with your parade of delicacies. I do hope you will enjoy." Brook did a slight bow and exited the room.

The table was round and large enough to seat six. Lucky pulled out a chair for Secret and assisted her in sitting. He then sat in the chair directly to her right.

"How are they going to begin bringing our food out when they haven't even shown us a menu and taken our orders?" Secret leaned in and whispered to Lucky as if the room had other patrons and she didn't want anyone to hear her.

"Because I took the liberty of ordering all the chef's specials in advance," Lucky informed her. "I know how chicks be acting on first dates, just trying to order salads and not eat. Well, I beat you to the punch. So much food is about to start coming to this table, you're not going to be able to resist eating."

"The sir is correct," a man wearing a white chef suit and hat said as he wheeled a cart of food over to their table. "But first allow your palate to be whetted by our best house wine."

The chef set a wineglass in front of each of them. He then pulled a bottle out of a glass ice-filled bucket and filled their glasses halfway. He then placed the ice bucket next to the vase.

Next the chef laid out four different appetizers that he named and described. "I'll give you two a few moments to indulge before I return with round two." He winked and then disappeared back into the kitchen.

Lucky picked up his glass. "Shall we toast?"

Secret stared at her glass, not bothering to pick it up.

"What's wrong? You don't like red wine. I can have him bring out white." Lucky immediately began calling for the chef. "Hey—"

"No, no, Lucky, it's not that." Secret stopped him.

"Then what is it?"

"Uh, I'm not old enough to drink. I'm only eighteen."

Lucky let out air between his lips and shooed his hand. "Oh, is that it?" Most people he knew had been drinking since middle school, so that wasn't a big deal to Lucky. "These mutherfuckers don't care how old you are as long as I pay the bill. They ain't trying to card nobody or nothing." He raised his glass again.

Secret was still resistant.

"What?"

"I . . . I don't drink." Not only didn't Secret drink, but she didn't want to start now that she was with child.

"Oh, snaps. I didn't know. I didn't even ask. My bad." Lucky wasn't used to this. All the girls he knew had been drinking since before half of them had even started their periods. He put his glass down.

"Please, you go ahead and drink up. Don't mind me. I'll just have—"

"Water. I forgot to bring your water out," the chef said. He was right on time as he held out two glasses of ice water with a slice of lemon and lime in each. "Please don't hold that against me."

"Thank you," Lucky said. "You're right on time actually."

The chef bowed and then once again disappeared.

"Okay, so now we can toast." Lucky once again lifted his glass of wine.

Secret lifted her glass of ice water. "So what do you want to toast to?"

Lucky thought for a moment. "To getting to know you better."

"Ditto," Secret said as the two clinked their glasses and then took sips of their drinks.

"So, uhhh, like I was saying before, are you from here?" Lucky asked Secret.

"Yep, born and raised," she told him, picking up one of the appetizers. She couldn't remember exactly what the chef had said it was, but to her, it was like an oval piece of mini garlic toast with tomato, cheese, and some other herbs. She took a bite. She chewed and swallowed then added, "But I didn't always live in Flint."

Secret proceeded to tell Lucky about herself, how she'd lived with her grandmother, her grandmother passing, et cetera. She found herself going on and on. The chef had come and gone about two or three more times with different choices of entrees each time. They'd sampled salads, soups, seafood, beef, chicken, and pastas. The chef had even whipped up a couple of nonalcoholic delights for Secret to indulge in upon Lucky's request.

By the time the chef brought out an array of desserts, three hours had passed and Secret had done most of the talking. She'd shared about her estranged relationship with her father, of course leaving out the details of her last visit with him. By the time they walked out of the bed and breakfast, they'd worked up a $1,500 tab, and that was on top of the fee he had to pay for reserving the dining room. They each felt like they'd gained five pounds. In addition, Lucky felt like he'd known Secret for the better part of her life, seeing she'd shared so much about herself with him.

"So did you enjoy yourself?" Lucky asked Secret as they walked down the walkway of the bed and breakfast and approached his truck.

"Oh my God, did I ever." Secret's eyes lit up. "For a first date ever, what more could a girl ask for?"

Lucky was about to open the door for Secret but then he paused. "You mean your first date with me."

Uh-oh, Secret thought. Shawndiece had spent so much time working with her so that she didn't come across as the rookie she was, and now here she'd gone off and spat the truth in spite of it all. "Uh, well."

Lucky turned Secret to face him. "You mean, no guy has ever taken you out on a date before?" He waited for a response that he never got. "Niggas can be such lames. All they wanna do is sit up with a chick but don't ever wanna spend money and take her out some place nice. Don't worry, sweetheart. You used to them young and dumb high school niggas who don't know how to date. You got you a real man now, so get prepared for more nights like this," Lucky told her, opening the door for her.

Secret only hoped he hadn't heard the huge gust of air she'd exhaled. He didn't think that she was some inexperienced pushover. He just thought she'd been with some lame, immature dudes who didn't know how to take a woman out. Shawdiece's efforts and teachings were not in vain after all.

Secret climbed up into her seat. She got nice and settled then realized Lucky was standing there just holding the door, staring at her. "What?" she asked.

He just shook his head. "I have no idea. I just got this feeling about you, girl."

"Oh, yeah," Secret said in a sassy manner, bobbing her head on her shoulders. "Well, I got a feeling about you too, Mr. Lucky."

"Oh, yeah?"

"Yeah."

"And what's that feeling?" he asked.

Secret thought for a moment. "That you really are going to be the right one." Secret didn't know much about Lucky. She didn't even have other guys to compare him with. But her instincts told her that he would be an excellent provider for her unborn baby.

"I feel that," Lucky said as he went to close the door.

Secret held her hand out. "Wait, you didn't tell me what feeling you have about me." Secret waited while Lucky stared into her eyes.

"I'm feeling like you the one I been trying to avoid."

That wasn't remotely close to what Secret was trying to hear. A frown covered her face to reflect her reaction to his response.

"No, no, I don't mean it like that," Lucky said. "I mean, keeping it real; I've kicked it with quite a few females. I love the female species. But I like to sample a lot of different flavors, as you can see by the menu I had arranged for us."

Secret nodded, still waiting for Lucky to make his point.

"I never wanted to be that dude who finds this one flavor he really likes, get hooked on it, and then lose his appetite for all the other tasty flavors out there. You know what I'm saying?"

"Yeah, I think I do." Secret turned her legs out of the car then used her index finger to signal Lucky to come in close.

He quickly looked to the side, licked his lips, smiled, then moved in close to Secret.

She immediately planted a soft, gentle kiss on his lips. She slowly slipped her tongue into his mouth. Before he could get into it and put his tongue to work, Secret pulled away. She then turned herself completely back in the vehicle, rested her hands on her knees, and looked straight ahead.

Lucky just stood there in a daze almost. It was almost like the roles were reversed. He was Snow White and had bitten the poisoned apple. Now here Secret had come along to kiss him on the lips and bring him back to life.

"What are you waiting for?" she turned and asked him. "You can take me home now."

"Are you serious? You just gon' pretend like you didn't just . . . I mean, what was all that for?"

"What? Oh, you mean the kiss?" Secret played dumb. "Well, that was just in case after tonight you decide you want to go dip your spoon into some other scoops of ice cream. I at least wanted you to have the aftertaste of my flavor to reminisce about." Secret faced forward again and waited for Lucky to close the door.

He ultimately did, but before he did he said, "You know what, Secret? Something tells me you're the cure to my sweet tooth." He closed the door and then did a light jog around the car to the driver's side.

Secret looked down at her stomach, then said to her unborn child, "Looks like Mommy has found you a daddy."

Chapter Sixteen

"You think just 'cause you eighteen and about to be a mama that you can come up in this motherfucker any time of night?" Yolanda spat as she sat on the couch watching television and smoking a cigarette.

"Ma, I'm sorry. I didn't realize it was this late," Secret said as she entered the house, closing the door behind her. It was almost two in the morning. Secret had never officially had a curfew because she never really went anywhere. She didn't even think about how her mother would react to her coming in at this kind of hour.

After Lucky had dropped Secret back off over Shawdiece's house, Shawndiece insisted Secret tell her every single detail about their date. Before Secret knew it, it was quarter to two in the morning. Shawdiece's mother had allowed her to borrow her car to take Secret home. Secret knew it was late but figured since she almost never went anywhere and never came in late, her mother wouldn't trip too much harder. On top of that, she was eighteen.

"Shawndiece and I went to the movies and then we went back to her house to talk about it and just got caught up." Secret couldn't believe how quickly that lie made its way between her lips. But more so, she couldn't believe how easy it came out. Being pregnant, forced into full-fledged adulthood, left Secret with little choice but to change. She not only had herself to look out for, but in a few months she'd have a little one to look out for as well.

As Secret stood there, she literally prayed to God that her mother would not ask her what movie the two had gone to see. She was quick on her feet, but not that quick.

"So you went to the movies with Shawndiece, huh?" her mother asked, slicing every inch of her with her eyes. "Shoulda known you was with that whore of a friend of yours. Now she even got you dressing like a whore. And since when can yo' ass walk in heels?"

Secret looked down at her shoes. "They're wedges."

"Heels, wedges, bitch, you know what the fuck I'm talking about. You always trying to prove to somebody how smart you are. Well, obviously there's somebody smarter than you:

the motherfucker who got that scholarship over yo' ass." Yolanda burst out laughing so hard she began to choke on her cigarette smoke.

"Fuck you."

Surely her mother had said those words because there is no way Secret had said them. She was thinking them, but no way under the sun could she have ever allowed them to slither from her brain, from her throat, and out of her mouth into her mother's ears. But by the way the world stopped spinning and her mother stared at her, it was obvious the words had somehow managed to escape into the universe.

"What the fuck you say?" Yolanda stood, adjusting her bra strap.

"I, uh, didn't mean to say it," Secret said, her heart beating so loud she was surprised she could hear her mother's voice over the continuous thump.

"Oh, don't be no punk now. Sure you meant to say the shit, else it wouldn't have come out your muthafuckin' throat." Yolanda began walking toward Secret. "You done got some dick up in you and think you the shit now. Dressed like you the shit. Talking like you the shit. Oh, you just a bad, grown-ass bitch now, huh?" Yolanda dipped back and then stood erect again.

"Mom, I'm sorry, I didn't mean to say it." As Yolanda closed in on Secret, she knew her mother was right. Being a punk wasn't about to get her anywhere. She'd said it and now she needed to own it. "I mean it; I just didn't mean to say it out loud because I never want to disrespect you."

"Bitch, you done already disrespected me by galanting in my house any time of night like you pay the bills."

"Gallivanting," Secret said under her breath.

"What?" Yolanda did a double take at her daughter.

"I think you meant to say the word 'gallivanting.' But I know what you meant," Secret tried to clean it up.

"I guess you saying to yourself, 'I know she 'bout to come bust me in my muthafuckin' mouth, so I might as well talk shit and give her something to really fuck me up over.'" Yolanda punched Secret in her mouth so fast that the blood from Secret's lip had already dripped to the floor before Secret even realized what happened.

"Mommy!" Secret yelled out in complete shock. She placed her hands over her mouth as her eyes filled with tears from the pain. Secret had become used to Yolanda's verbal abuse and being knocked upside the head every now and then. But her mother going to extremes and getting physical with her like some stranger on the street stunned her heart.

"Don't 'Mommy' me. Grown bitches don't holler out for they mommy. Now talk some more shit, ho. You think just 'cause you pregnant I won't floor your ass. Keep running that mouth."

"I can't believe you just hit me like that while I'm pregnant with your grandchild," Secret cried. "Grandmother would have never done that."

Yolanda being compared to her mother made her blood boil over and out the pot. Before she knew it, she'd hauled off and swung on Secret, this time the punch landing on Secret's side. She swung yet again, but this time Secret was able to stop her by grabbing hold of her wrist.

"Oh, not only do you wanna run your mouth," Yolanda hollered, "but now you wanna put your hands on me, too. Oh, you really need me to shut your ass down."

Yolanda tussled with Secret until they ended up on the ground. Yolanda managed to loosen one of her wrists from Secret's grip. As she yanked her wrist from Secret's hand, Secret's nails sliced down her arm. In pain and anger, Yolanda grabbed Secret by the

hair and began slamming her head into the
floor. Secret grabbed hold of her mother's
wrist again, trying to pull her hands from her
head, but she wasn't strong enough.

"Stop it! Stop it!" Secret cried out. She kicked
and twisted underneath her mother as she
kicked and scrubbed her feet on the ground in a
desperate attempt to free herself.

After what felt like forever, Secret managed
to muster up a heap of strength, buck her body,
and flip her mother off of her. In a flash, Secret
was on her feet and back out of the house.
Secret didn't look back as she raced down the
sidewalk.

"And, bitch, if you think you ever coming back
here, you got another think coming," Yolanda
yelled from the porch. "Gon' disrespect me like I
ain't gave you life."

Secret walked down the street crying like a
baby as she listened to her mother call her every
whore, tramp, ho, and bitch there was. Secret
had long been immune to her mother's rage,
temper, and verbal insults. But now it wasn't
just about her anymore. Now she had another
living being to look after, and as far as she was
concerned, there was no worse way her mother
could have violated her than to attack her while
she was pregnant.

"She could have killed my baby," Secret called out as she was walking in them wedges as if she'd been wearing them all her life. Her adrenaline was all the way turned up. She made it to Shawdiece's house in record time.

She walked up to Shawdiece's double-family home and knocked on the door. Only a few seconds went by, but it felt like hours as she knocked on the door again, harder this time.

"I bet whoever it is betta be the ma'fuckin' police knocking on my shit this time of night like that."

Secret could hear Shawdiece's mother's voice from the other side of the door.

"I'm sorry, Ms. Franklin," Secret immediately apologized once Shawndiece's mother opened the door. "Is Shawndiece here?"

"What?" Ms. Franklin eagerly stuck her head out the door and looked around. "She s'posed to be dropping you off. Why you back here and where the fuck she at with my car?" She threw her hands on her hips. "I don't know what kind of game you two are playing, but y'all lucky I got company and ain't had none in a minute or I'd be in both y'all asses." Ms. Franklin stepped back inside. "When you find Shawndiece, tell her she better fill my tank up; playing games with me."

Secret stood on the porch stunned as Ms. Franklin closed the door in her face and went back to entertain her company.

Secret began to cry again as she buried her face in her hands. "Oh God. I can't believe this," she cried. "What am I going to do?" Secret had no idea what her next step was going to be. What she did know was that she could not, she would not, step foot in her mother's house ever again.

She sat down on the steps. Even though it was summer, there was a chill in the night air. She pulled her knees to her chest and wrapped her arms around her legs. She knew she had to come up with something. She couldn't sit on her best friend's porch all night and freeze to death. And if she knocked on Ms. Franklin's door again and interrupted her getting her groove on, she'd probably do worse damage to Secret than her mother had already done.

As snot dripped from Secret's nose, she dug into her purse to get a tissue. She felt around and that's when she pulled out the answer to solve her dilemma.

Chapter Seventeen

Secret was beginning to think that her best friend was right; perhaps she really did need a cell phone. She needed a phone right now more than anything. From the looks of things, they just didn't make pay phones anymore.

"You all right?" Secret heard a voice ask her as she exited the gas station lot. She'd gone there hoping to find a pay phone on the grounds but had no such luck.

"No, I'm good," Secret said on instinct. It was the middle of the night. Good people weren't out lurking in the middle of the night unless they were up to no good. Then she thought for a second. Heck, she was out lurking in the middle of the night and she wasn't up to no good.

"Actually," Secret said as she turned around to face a woman who was pumping her gas. "Do you happen to have a cell phone I can use?"

"Sure. Hold on a sec. It's on the car charger." The woman, dressed in scrubs as if she worked in a hospital, finished up pumping her gas and put the nozzle back. "You bold to be out here in the middle of the night in a mini skirt," the woman said to Secret. "Figure it wasn't by choice, especially with that distressed look on your face like you've lost your best friend." She went and opened up her car door. She reached in, grabbed her cell phone, and then handed it to Secret.

Speaking of best friend, that's exactly who Secret planned on calling. If Shawndiece was still out in her mother's car, she could come swoop her up. She dialed her best friend's cell phone. She was excited to hear it ring, but her excitement was short-lived, murdered to be exact, when it went straight to voice mail after just one ring.

Secret sighed heavily. She dialed again and again it went straight to voice mail. Shawdiece's phone was apparently turned off.

"No answer?" the woman surmised. "Is there anyone else you can call or somewhere I can drop you off at?"

Secret closed her eyes and tried to think hard about who else she could call. After just a few seconds, her eyes opened, full of renewed hope. She reached in her purse and pulled out the piece of paper she'd been fondling earlier while on Shawdiece's porch. She proceeded to punch the numbers from the piece of paper into the borrowed cell phone.

"Yo," Secret heard a voice say.

"Hey." She hesitated in her response.

"Secret?"

"Uh, yeah, hey," she said, looking down, away from the good Samaritan who was staring down her throat.

"What's going on, girl? Let me guess; your little plan backfired. You done got a taste of me and now you got midnight cravings?" Lucky's laugh flowed through the receiver, putting a half smile on Secret's face for the first time in a minute.

"Something like that, I guess you could say." Secret tried her best to keep her voice from cracking, but she couldn't help it. Lucky's voice was like a safety net right now that she just wanted to fall into. She just hoped by calling him she wouldn't look desperate or that it would turn him off when he learned the truth about her home life.

"You okay?" Concern trimmed out Lucky's words.

Secret paused, swallowing tears. "I hate to call on you, but I wouldn't if I really didn't—"

"Yo, you can call on me whenever. What's up?"

Where was Shawndiece when Secret really needed her? Certainly her friend would have been able to feed her some quick lie to share with Lucky. All Secret had was the truth. She prayed the truth wouldn't make Lucky think she was this little girl with issues with her mommy at home. What man would want to deal with that kind of drama? Well, she had no choice but to find out. "I kind of got into it with my mom and she put me out." Secret ran her hand down her hair, realizing for the first time that it was in total disarray. She had no idea she'd been walking around with her hair standing on top of her head like she was one of those Treasure Troll dolls she used to play with when she was little. "I tried to call Shawndiece to come pick me up, but—"

"Where are you?" Lucky interrupted her for the second time.

Secret quickly put her hand over her mouth to hold in the cry that wanted to yelp out. She was so touched that Lucky was willing to help her without hesitating. Her eyes watered and the owner of the cell phone rested her hand on her shoulder, letting her know it would be okay. She then voiced her gesture. "Li'l Muffin, it's going to be all right." The woman smiled, her comforting reassurance putting a smile on Secret's face, enabling her to pull herself together and finish her conversation with Lucky.

Secret looked around at the street signs and then told Lucky where she was.

"Cool. You inside the gas station? You using their phone?"

"No, this lady let me use her cell phone. I'm outside."

"Well, go inside and wait for me. I'm on the other side of town, so it's gonna take me a minute. Go inside and wait," Lucky repeated for good measure.

Secret nodded as if Lucky could see her sign for understanding through the phone. "Okay." Secret ended the phone call and then handed the phone back to the woman. "Thank you so much. I really appreciate it. My friend is on his way. I'm going to go wait inside."

"Fine. I'll wait with you," the woman offered.

"Oh, you don't have to do that," Secret told her. "It's late." She pointed to her. "And it looks like you either just got off work or are headed to work."

"Just got off," the woman informed her. "Oh, by the way, I'm Ray. That's what my friends call me. It's short for Raygiene." The woman extended her hand to Secret.

"Thank you, Ray." Secret shook her hand. "But really you don't have to wait. I'll be fine. My friend will be here in a minute."

"You sure? Because I don't mind. Really, I don't. Pretty girl like yourself out here dressed like you're about to hit the runway . . ."

Once again, Secret smiled. "Thank you." She knew the woman was just being nice, trying to comfort her. She looked a hot mess and she knew it. "But you've done plenty. I'll be fine." Secret thanked Ray again and then made her way inside the gas station.

She went to the bathroom to straighten herself up a little before Lucky arrived. Even after she'd used the bathroom and got herself together, she waited inside a little longer. She'd rather wait in there than stand out in the gas station looking like a hooker waiting for her pimp to come scoop her up.

After about twenty minutes, Secret made her way out of the bathroom. She crossed her fingers that when she looked out the gas station door she'd see Lucky's truck, but she didn't. She did see something else that put a surprised look on her face. Secret smiled and waved.

Ray, who stood outside leaning against her car, waved back.

Secret shook her head. She couldn't believe this complete stranger had thought so much about her safety as to wait and look out for her. A horn tore Secret from her thoughts. Her eyes darted to see Lucky's SUV pulling up in front of the door. Secret hurried and exited out the door at the same time Lucky was getting out of his truck. He made it to the passenger's side just in time to open the door for Secret.

"You all ri—"

Before Lucky could even get his complete sentence out of his mouth, Secret threw her arms around his neck. "Thank you so much for coming. I hope you don't think I'm some chick with drama, but . . ." Secret's words trailed off when Lucky pulled away and placed his index finger over her slightly swollen lips.

"Ma, I know drama, and this ain't shit," he told her. "Come on. Get in." He opened the door for her, waited until she was nice and situated, and then closed the door. He walked around to the driver's side and got in. He then looked at Secret and said, "Where to?"

She looked down. She hadn't thought that far in advance. She just knew that she needed to get off the streets. "I can't go home," was all she said.

Lucky put the vehicle in drive. "Don't worry, I got you."

As they pulled off, Secret thought about Ray and wanted to give a thank-you wave. But as they drove away, she realized Ray had already driven away and was nowhere in sight.

Secret sat back in the seat with her seat belt on. She had no idea where she was going, but was just glad to be going somewhere other than home. She looked down at her stomach.

I might not make it out of the hood, little one, but I'll be damned if you don't!

Chapter Eighteen

Lucky didn't say too much to Secret as they drove. He figured whatever information she wanted to share with him, she would. After about ten minutes of driving, Lucky pulled up into a Walmart. It was at a crazy hour, so there were quite a few available parking spaces close to the door. Lucky pulled into one and turned off the engine.

"If it was a decent time, you know Walmart wouldn't be quite the place I would have liked to have taken you to on a shopping spree," Lucky said.

"What?" Secret's thoughts had been preoccupied with the fight she'd just had with her mother. She hadn't even paid attention to the fact that they'd even pulled into a Walmart.

Lucky repeated himself. Secret still just sat there looking at him without understanding.

"You're gonna need some stuff to get you through the night, the next couple of days, or whatever. Right?"

Secret's thoughts became clear as she looked over to the store entrance. Realizing where she was at and what Lucky had just said, she put two and two together. "Oh, yeah, but . . . I, uhhh . . ."

She had to think quickly. She didn't have any money. Her dilemma with coming up with a lie, though, was that she was already lying by omission by keeping the fact that she was pregnant from Lucky. That was enough to keep up with. If she continued to lie, she'd end up getting caught in her own trap. She didn't want to take that chance, so the truth it was.

Secret turned her body to face Lucky. "Look, Lucky, my focus has been on school, getting good grades so I could make something of myself. I don't have a job. My mom looked out for me. So you can just pull off." She turned back to look straight ahead. There, she'd said. She was broke and now homeless. What?

Lucky didn't say a word. He just got out of the car, walked around to the passenger's side, and opened the door. He stood there.

"What?" Secret said.

"Get out, that's what," Lucky told her in just as crabby of a voice as she had used.

"I said I don't have any money."

Lucky closed his eyes, put his head down, and swung it from left to right. "You just don't get it do you?" He lifted his head and looked at Secret. "Ma, you fuckin' with a real nigga now. Now let me be that nigga and take you up in here and get you what you gon' need." Lucky took Secret by the hand and pulled her out of the car.

Secret slowly got out. She stood there and looked up at the Walmart sign while Lucky closed the door behind her. The timid and inexperienced side of Secret began to surface. Shawndiece hadn't told her how to act when a guy basically took her by the hand into a store and told her to run free like a kid at Toys "R" Us. Her eyes were sparkling with excitement. Then she remembered something Shawndiece had told her.

"And don't be lookin' and actin' all thirsty or else he might know something's up," Shawndiece had said.

Secret quickly blinked away the excitement in her eyes so that Lucky wouldn't mistake it for greed. She walked side by side with Lucky into the store. After about an hour, they came out of the store, each carrying bags of everything Secret might need to hold her for a couple of days or so. Toiletries, a pack of underwear, bras, pajamas, a couple outfits, a pair of shoes, and other miscellaneous items.

"Thank you. I really appreciate this," Secret said. "I'll pay you back."

"Oh, yeah, how?" Lucky asked with just a light sheet of confusion covering his face.

Secret stopped in her tracks. Lucky took a few more steps before he realized that Secret was no longer beside him. He turned around to find her standing with her hands on her hips, bags dangling from each arm.

"What?" he asked.

"Pay you back, huh? Mr. I Got You, Let Me Be a Man." Secret sucked her teeth. "Oh, you a man all right. Buy a chick a couple items and now she gotta pay you back with some sex?" She let out a harrumph. "Well, if that's what you think this is about, you can march this stuff all the way back into the store and return it."

"Is that what you thought I meant by that?" Lucky laughed. "I mean how you gon' pay me back when you just said that you didn't have a job."

If Secret's hands weren't full of bags, she would have been able to pick up her face off the ground. She felt real stupid. "Oh. I'm sorry."

Lucky laughed. "You snapped off on me. I didn't know you had it in you. You sure underneath all that good-girl exterior there ain't the real you, a hood chick, waiting to jump out?" He took off walking again.

Secret chuckled. "You crazy." She followed Lucky. "And no, there isn't. What you see is what you get." Under her breath she added, "And a little bit more."

They loaded the bags into the car. Once they were both settled back into the SUV, Lucky drove for about another twenty minutes before they pulled up to a hotel. Secret noticed on the sign that they offered weekly rates.

"You can wait in here while I go make sure they have a room available. Then we can lug all this stuff in." He got out of the car and disappeared into the hotel building. After about ten minutes he returned and got back in the car. "Your room is around the other side." He started the truck and drove to the side of the building. They got all the bags from the car and Lucky guided them to a side door where he had to swipe his hotel-issued key card for them to enter.

Once inside they took the elevator to the fourth floor and went to room 416. "Here we go." Lucky slid the key card down the strip, opened the door, and let Secret enter.

"Hold up right there," Secret said, dropping her bags and walking past Lucky as he stood at the door, holding it open for her. She walked inside and went straight to the bathroom. She pulled the shower curtain open and looked behind it. She then went and looked in the closet, under the beds, and anywhere else she thought could hold a warm-blooded body. She felt that it was safe to say that there was no one else in the room besides her and Lucky. "Okay; we good." She picked up her bags and carried them into her king suite with a kitchenette.

"What the hell was all that about?" Lucky snickered.

"I had to make sure nobody was up in here who isn't supposed to be."

"See, I knew I was right about you. You are different. You sweet, innocent, and smart and all, but you got some street smarts about you, too," Lucky said. "Something tells me you done dealt with enough knuckleheads to know what's up."

Secret wasn't sure how she felt about that last comment of Lucky's. She cringed at the thought that he even thought she had experience with lots of other guys. That wasn't the case at all, so it was time to set him straight.

"Well, you have Shawndiece to thank for that," Secret admitted, plopping down on the bed. "In all honesty. I don't date. I don't really deal with dudes at all. I live vicariously through my best friend."

Lucky set down the bags he was carrying and went and sat down next to Secret. "You serious or are you just trying to make me think you ain't fast?"

"I'm serious."

"So you mean if I have a gang load of friends, I don't have to worry about you having had smashed the homies?"

Secret pulled her head back. "What are you talking about?"

Lucky just sat there and stared at Secret like he'd never seen anything like her in his life. Truth be told, he hadn't. Girls like Kat and Tanesha: a dime a dozen. Girls like Secret: priceless. If the fellas ever caught wind of this ripe princess, they'd make it their business to try to get at her. That's why he knew now more than ever that Secret would be just that: his little Secret.

Chapter Nineteen

The sun was bound and determined to get Secret's attention by forcing its way through the small slither of a crack in the hotel room curtains. Secret had to admit, though, that being kissed by the morning sun was a great thing to wake up to.

She sat up and realized she was on the king-sized bed. She was under the cover but fully clothed. She sat and thought for a minute, trying to replay the final moments of the wee morning hours before she'd fallen off to sleep. A smile crept across her lips the same way the sun's ray had crept into her room.

"Lucky." The word slipped through her lips like chocolate sliding down a chocoholic's throat. She lay back down as a smile took over her very being.

She remembered Lucky helping her get her things from Walmart situated and giving her the security of knowing he'd booked the king room for an entire week. "Hopefully you and your moms will get stuff straightened out by then, but if not, just know I got you."

Secret had never met anyone so kind, caring, and giving toward her in her life; not since her grandmother. Not that she'd ever really made it a point to get out there and mingle and get to know folks like Shawndiece did.

"Shawndiece." Both that word and Secret shot up like a rocket. Secret excitedly looked to her left and then to her right in search of a phone. She went to pick it up but was interrupted by a knock on the door.

Secret got up out of the bed with a peculiar look on her face. Who could be at the door? Nobody knew she was there except for, "Lucky," her lips formed to say as she picked up her pace and raced to the door. "Who is it?" she decided to ask for GP as well as look through the peephole.

"Room service," the Mexican woman she was staring at through the peephole replied.

Secret opened the door to find the woman standing behind a cart full of food.

"Just like the mister requested. Breakfast served at eleven," the woman said to Secret as she positioned the cart to enter the hotel room.

Secret stepped aside and allowed the woman to wheel the cart in. She eyeballed fresh fruit, a glass of orange juice, apple juice, and what was either pineapple juice or grapefruit juice. There were waffles, pancakes, crepes, and French toast. There were scrambled eggs, an omelet, and quiche. Secret's mouth watered at the country potatoes smothered in onion with hunks of polish sausage. The biscuits covered in sausage and gravy looked tasty, too. There were a couple choices of cold cereals and a small pitcher of milk, as well as a mini coffee pot and a miniature-size kettle with hot water and a variety of teas.

"When you are finished, you can just place the cart in the hall and someone will get it. I do hope you enjoy." The woman went to walk away.

"Uh, ma'am, this all does look delicious, but I, uh, didn't order it." Secret felt embarrassed. "And I kind of don't have the money to pay for it either."

"Like I said, the mister ordered. It's been charged to the credit card on file at the front desk. Gratuity has already been added as well." The woman nodded and left the room, the door closing and locking automatically behind her.

Secret stared at the delicacies for a moment before pinching herself and then laughing at her own lame gesture. "What, oatmeal too?" she noticed. "That boy is too much. Or should I say man; real man," she said almost mocking Lucky.

Secret picked up a waffle that was smothered in melting butter and took a bite as if she were eating a slice of pizza. She's planned to sit down and indulge but had to go to the restroom first.

After using the bathroom, she couldn't wash her hands fast enough and get back out there to all the food that awaited her. Just as she was halfway into the sitting area, the hotel room phone rang. Her smile lit up the room. She knew it was Lucky because he was the only one who knew where she was. "Right on time," she said, figuring she needed to thank him for the room service. "You're right. I've never been with a real man before, not like you," Secret said, falling back on the bed and twisting the phone cord like she was in la-la land while talking to her high school sweetheart.

"Bitch, how you gon' be sounding all like you in heaven and shit and I'm over here worried sick, 'bout to sic Rashad and his boys on Lucky?"

"Shawndiece?" Secret's sweet, lovey-dovey mood was instantly shattered.

"Uh, yes? What? You wasn't gon' call a bitch and let her know where you was at? I called your house after I got in and my mom told me you'd been by the house looking for me. Your mom was cussing and fussing talking about she put that ho out. Blah blah blah. I didn't know what to think.

I kept calling your house, pissing your mom off. Me and her ended up having words. I was worried sick about your ass. Ain't slept all fuckin' night. Then I gets to thinking how you called Lucky from my phone. I gotta go through my call log and shit. That nigga answered the phone; I'm so on edge that a bitch just go in on his ass. I'm telling that nigga I'ma fuck his shit up and his mama gon' report his ass missin' if my girl don't turn up in an hour. Then this nigga tell me you chillin' out in a hotel somewhere like you's fuckin' Paris Hilton or some shit and ain't bothered to call me, knowing I was gon' be worried sick about you."

There was a few seconds of silence. "Hello to you too," Secret finally spoke, realizing Shawndiece had finally decided to take a break from cursing her out.

"Bitch, don't play with me." Shawndiece sounded genuinely upset.

"Aww, boo-boo, you was really worried about me like that?" Secret teased, while at the same time her heart was touched. She'd bet her firstborn her mama went into work like normal and didn't think twice about her.

"Ain't nobody playing with yo' ass, Secret." Shawndiece was much too hard to allow her sensitive side to show, but Secret could hear in her voice Shawndiece really had been scared for her.

"Look, I'm sorry. I really am. My mom went off on me; I mean literally tried to kill me, Shawndiece," Secret began to explain. "You know you all I got, so I came straight to your house. But you weren't there. I even tried to call you after that."

"I made a couple stops since I had my mom's car," Shawndiece said in an apologetic tone. She'd calmed down some.

"I figured that," Secret said. "I didn't have anybody else to call but Lucky."

"I'm just glad he came through for you," Shawndiece said, exhaling for the first time, sounding like she was ready to have a normal conversation with her best friend.

"Girl, he came through like you wouldn't believe." Secret began telling Shawndiece about how Lucky stopped her off at Walmart, to him getting her the hotel room for a week, right down to the buffet of breakfast foods that awaited her in the next room.

"Well, did you give him some pussy for all that?" Shawndiece spat out.

"Girl, no. He didn't even try to go there with me."

"Well, trust and believe that nigga will be back through to collect. So get yo' ass off the phone with me, go eat up some of that food, then get your ass in the shower and go put on them Tweety Bird pajamas you got from Wally World."

Secret laughed. "Girl, they ain't no Tweety Bird pajamas."

"Well, whatever they are, make 'em sexy. Have your ass smelling good and spread out like his smorgasbord. Bam! Next thing you know, you calling that nigga in a couple weeks talkin' 'bout 'you are the father.'"

"Girl, bye," Secret said, planning to take heed of Shawndiece's instructions no matter how undiplomatic she was in relaying them.

"Bye. Call me after you do him."

"Girl, bye!" Secret hung up the phone and took another bite of her waffle. She sat there for a minute just smiling and thinking about her bestie. She was so touched that Shawndiece had cared so much about her that she'd called around looking for her. Secret knew one thing for certain: she and Shawndiece would be friends for life . . . no matter what.

For the next hour, Secret watched television while sampling almost every food and beverage room service had brought to her. Afterward, she took a shower and got herself smelling good with some of the products she'd bought from the store last night.

She was going to call Lucky but decided she would just wait for him to check in on her. She didn't want to seem all clingy. A couple hours went by and she hadn't heard from him. That was a little disappointing to Secret because he seemed like the type who would have checked in on her by now. This was a sign that Secret was falling for this guy and his chivalry from the night before really cemented that. But now that he hadn't called, she was getting nervous that he didn't feel the same way about her. As she began to question whether perhaps she was more into him than he was into her, she had to remind herself of what really mattered: him ultimately being into the child growing inside her stomach.

He could be busy at work for all I know, Secret told herself to appease her anxiety of not having heard from him. But when another couple of hours went by, she was feeling almost abandoned.

Was this guy a joke, just putting on a show, saying what he thought she wanted him to say and doing what he thought she wanted him to do? For all she knew, he could be another Rolland from back in the day and have a family he was taking care of somewhere. Her stomach turned at the thought that she really would, in fact, be living her mother's life. At six o'clock, there was another knock on the door.

Butterflies fluttered all through Secret's stomach as she jumped up off the couch. She knew this had to be Lucky. If she would just be real with herself, baby or no baby, she was excited about just simply being in Lucky's presence.

"Finally," she said under her breath as she padded in bare feet to the door. Before opening it, she patted down the Jersey-like short nightgown that had the number twelve in hot pink written across the front. She'd put her hair back in a slick ponytail, but patted it down as well to make sure not a hair was out of place. "About time," she said in a teasing voice as she flung open the hotel room door.

"Sorry, ma'am. The ticket said six o'clock. It's six o'clock."

This time it was a white man standing behind a cart full of various types of food.

"Oh, I'm sorry," Secret apologized, feeling stupid and slighted by her so-called Prince Charming. She stepped to the side and opened the door for the man to bring the cart in.

He pushed the cart in, giving her the same instruction with this cart as the Mexican woman

had given her with the cart that held the breakfast foods.

"Yes, I'll be sure to put it out in the hallway,"
Secret assured him as she followed him to the
door and closed it behind him.

She didn't even race over to the cart to see
what edible delights it held. She didn't have an
appetite. She was almost starting to feel like she
was in prison, cut off from the rest of the world,
being fed three meals a day. Of course they
didn't get served food like this in prison. Still,
Secret felt as if her fairytale was already ending.
No, she wasn't being held hostage or anything.
Surely she could leave the walls of the hotel
room, but then she'd risk missing Lucky. She
had it bad.

Before she could flop down in a pout on the
couch, there was a knock at the door again.
Secret sighed and stomped her feet back to
the door. She figured room service must have
forgotten to leave something. "Yes," Secret said,
yanking open the door.

Secret had to fight back tears as she saw Lucky
standing there with three dozen red roses.

"You didn't think I was going to let you eat
dinner alone, did you?"

Chapter Twenty

By the time Secret realized what she had done, it was too late. She'd already moved the roses out of the way, flung her arms around his neck, and shoved her tongue down his throat. Lucky couldn't even speak. He couldn't even breathe. Secret was so deep into him that she was breathing for him; thank God!

Lucky backed her into the room, still kissing her. Once the hotel room door closed, after Lucky gave it a little assistance by kicking it with his foot, he dropped the flowers and wrapped his arms around Secret.

The two stood in the middle of the hotel room kissing as if Lucky had been away at war for years and was just returning home. From the outside looking in, no one would have been able to tell that the couple hadn't even known each other for a week. They were so intertwined they could be mistaken for one.

Once the two finally decided to come up for air, they just pulled apart from each other and stood there eyeing one another. No words were spoken but enough was being said, enough for Secret to lift her nightgown over her head and stand there in nothing but some lavender lace-trimmed panties. Her perky nipples stared at Lucky, beckoning him to caress them, and then moisten them with his lips, which was exactly what he did.

First Lucky cupped her breasts in his hands and then one by one teased them with the tip of his tongue. Secret allowed her head to fall back and just take all of his touch in. Next, she took him by the hands and walked backward, escorting him to the king-sized bed. Once they reached the bed, looking him in his eyes, Secret slid the panties down her hips and allowed them to land at her ankles. She stepped out of them and right onto the bed. She lay there, wide open, her womanhood calling for Lucky to enter her walls.

Licking his lips and forcing himself to take his time, Lucky began to disrobe until he was naked on top of Secret, and then inside her.

"Ooooohhhhh." Secret's moan was a cross between ecstasy and pain. Her body wasn't quite used to being entered like this. Slowly but surely, though, it accepted Lucky's vessel into its body of water. "Ummmmmm." It was becoming more enjoyable with each rock of the boat.

"You feel so good," Lucky whispered in her ear as he slowly dipped in and out of Secret. She just lay there and allowed him to do most of the work, but he didn't mind. She was open for him and greeting him with a warm welcome. He got lost inside of Secret. It wasn't the sexy, off-the-chain, "do whatever you want to me" sex Lucky was used to having, the last hood rat trying to outdo the next. This was different. Everything about Secret was different. He couldn't tell himself that enough.

It was still daylight outside. It was light inside. Secret didn't care. She didn't care that Lucky could see every inch of her body and anything he might deem as a flaw. She had no cares in the world right about now. She'd never dreamed of experiencing what she was experiencing with Lucky. Yes, she had been genuinely attracted to him that day at the clinic. Yes, she might have decided to give him a call for selfish reasons, but at the end of the day, Secret could honestly say that baby or no baby, Lucky was someone she wouldn't mind having in her life. So not only was that like a bonus, but it was also good for her conscience as well.

As Lucky thrust himself in and out of her secret hiding place, he lifted Secret's legs so that with each thrust, the heels of her feet tapped his ass cheeks. Faster, quicker, deeper until they were both moaning and they both finally exploded. Lucky just lay there, his sweat dripping onto Secret's body that rested under him.

"Girl, you are dangerous." Lucky finally removed himself from inside of and off of Secret and lay beside her.

"Why you say that?" Secret asked, staring up at the ceiling.

He turned and looked at her. "You could have a nigga catching feelings and shit," he admitted.

"Quit playing," Secret said as she turned and looked to him. "You know you already feel some kind of way." She looked into the area where the food cart sat. "Or do you do this type of thing for every girl you just meet?"

Lucky put his hands behind his head. "Hell no. These bitches out here is thirsty, scandalous. They begging and asking for shit before you could ever get a chance to even want to do something nice. They got this level of expectancy or something like that."

"Entitlement," Secret said.

"Yeah, entitlement," Lucky agreed. "Like the world owes them something."

Secret stared back up at the ceiling. "It's funny, most of us come from nothing, yet expect everything, but aren't willing to work for anything."

Lucky paused for a minute. "That's real talk right there."

"Oh, yeah?"

"Yeah."

Secret turned her attention back to Lucky. "Speaking of work, I have to find me a j-o-b." Secret sighed. "I can't live in a hotel forever. Even if I could, I couldn't afford to."

Lucky went to open his mouth, but Secret cut him off.

"And before you even say anything, I know you got me. But I'm eighteen now. I need to have myself."

Lucky sat up in bed. "I feel you on that. I wanna see you doing your independent woman thang. Like I said, you got it going on in so many ways other broads out here don't. You're special. Other broads need to see a chick like you make it. Need some motivation in their life."

"You sure do place me on a high pedestal without even hardly knowing who I am."

Lucky leaned over to get up close and personal with Secret. "I don't care that I don't know who you are really. I'm a pretty good judge of character, so what really matters is that I know who you are not." Lucky kissed Secret on the lips and then went into the bathroom.

After hearing the toilet flush, Secret heard the shower come on. She sat up in bed just when Lucky peeked his head out of the bathroom. "Wanna join me in the shower?"

"I thought you'd never ask." Secret got out of the bed and joined Lucky in the shower where they took turns washing each other's backs.

They were intimate, but not in a sexual way. It was hard to describe, but it was safe to say that a connection had been made in the shower just as much as it had been made in the king-sized bed, where neither one of them would ever admit that they'd made love.

"You two good?" Lucky asked Shawndiece and Secret as he prepared to leave the hotel room.

"Yeah, baby, we good," Secret replied as she walked over and gave him a kiss on the cheek. "Thanks for taking me to get my stuff."

"Yeah, thank you," Shawndiece cut in. "'Cause I thought I was about to catch a case trying to keep them hounds from taking your shit after Ms. Yolanda set it all out on the curb."

That morning Secret had received a frantic call from Shawndiece telling her that her mother had called her informing her that she'd set all Secret's stuff out on the curb. She'd been under the impression that Secret was staying with Shawndiece and Shawndiece didn't tell her otherwise. She just picked up the phone and called Secret as she hauled tail over to Secret's house to guard her stuff until Secret could come pick it up. Secret could hear Shawndiece fighting off the leeches in the background when she called to relay the news.

Thank God Lucky had been there to take her to go get her things. After loading up his Escalade, all three went back to the hotel. After getting a 911 text from Major Pain, Lucky was now on his way out the door to take care of business, something he'd neglected to do the past few days, opting to stay up under Secret instead.

"Be safe out there," Secret said to Lucky as he exited the hotel room. She closed the door, turned around, leaned against the door, and just stared off for a minute. She smiled and then sashayed over to join Shawndiece on the couch.

"Bitch, that nigga got you wide open. I can tell," Shawndiece said, staring at Secret. "Damn, Secret, girl; is it like that?"

"Shawndiece, girl. I hate to admit it, but I'm really feeling Lucky," Secret confessed.

"Hell, I can tell. You got stars and shit in your eyes. I know it just ain't the pregnancy glow. Speaking of pregnancy . . ." Shawndiece scooted in closer to Secret. "I know you been lettin' that nigga hit that. He done hit it raw so you can handle yo' business, right?"

Secret threw her head back. "It's not even like that, Shawn."

"You can tell yourself that so you can sleep at night, but we both know that's exactly what it's about. You remember why you need this nigga in your life. If you fall in love with him for real, hell, that's just a plus. But don't fuck this up by letting your emotions get in the way. In two weeks, tell that nigga you missed your period and get the ball rolling, then you good to go. Fall in love, get married. Fuck, have a bunch of babies. Just do what you need to do for this one right here." She pointed to Secret's belly.

"I know, I know. You don't have to keep reminding me what the ultimate goal is." Secret stood and stomped over to the kitchenette. She grabbed a juice from the fridge, cracked it open, and took a swig.

Shawndiece let out a deep breath. She got up off the couch and went and met Secret in the kitchenette. "Look, Secret, I know this is hard for you. You ain't cut out like the rest of us in the hood, but, baby girl, when you're back is up against the wall, you got to use every muscle to make shit happen." She grabbed Secret's crotch. "And that means your pussy muscle, too."

Secret slapped Shawndiece's hand away and went and flopped back down on the couch.

"Everything is going to work out, Secret. Just keep it together. I'm here for you every step of the way. It's all going to work out. You hear me?"

Secret, trying to remove all doubt from her tone, replied, "Yes, I hear you." Hearing it was the easy part. Believing it would be a whole other thing.

Chapter Twenty-one

"Nigga, what the fuck? Trying to get a hold of your ass the last few days has been like trying to figure out where the fuck Jimmy Hoffa is at." Major Pain could hardly control his temper as he got in the passenger's seat of Lucky's Escalade.

"Man, shut up and get yo' ass in the car," Lucky said, already expecting to get the business from Major. For the last few days Lucky had been MIA from the world. Time must really fly when you're having fun, because he was losing track of the days due to the fact he was having so much fun spending time with Secret.

In the last four days Lucky had gotten Secret a cell phone, and talked with Secret about taking her to pick out a nice reliable used car so that she could go job hunting. It was clear, after her mother put all her stuff out on the curb, that she was officially now on her own. She'd have to put all the independent woman stuff in motion. Strangely enough, Lucky felt good spending dough on and taking care of Secret. For the first time since he could remember, he felt like someone in this world really needed him. Secret asked for nothing, yet he was willing to give her anything. Lucky felt that he was turning into what his boys would have referred to as a sucker. Which was why there was no way he was going to tell them he'd hooked up with this shorty who he was giving all his time to.

"I had a family emergency, ma'fucka," was the lie Lucky told Major Pain. He didn't actually feel like he was lying though. Secret felt like family, something Lucky knew nothing about. His dope-addicted, jailed parents had only made him. The streets had raised him.

"But your phone still worked, right, nigga?" Major spat as he slammed the door after getting in the passenger's seat.

"Yo, man, watch my fuckin' door." He looked at Major Pain, who was looking straight ahead with his lip poked out. "Man, is you one of my bitches or you my ride or die nigga? Over there lookin' like one of them hoes I be fuckin' wit'." Lucky shook his head and pulled off.

"Nigga, fuck you!"

"You act like you are fucking me. If you didn't like pussy so much, I'd think you had a crush on a nigga." Lucky started batting his eyes and rubbed Major Pain on his knee.

"Man, fuck you!" Major Pain spat before a smile forced itself on his lips. "For real, though, man. I been holding shit down. But you know how these li'l niggas get when they don't see your face around for a minute. They think they can start slipping and dippin'. I ain't trying to have no more Aces on our hands." He looked over to Lucky. "You feel me, my nigga?"

"Yeah, I feel you, which is why I called yo' ass so we can go make some rounds today. Like I said, my bad for being MIA, but some shit came up that I had to handle."

"Well, is that shit handled?" Major Pain shot him a serious look. "You need me to take care of some things for you?" He patted his gat he had tucked down in his waist.

"Naw, I'm good. But good looking out."

Major Pain nodded. There was brief silence before he spoke again. "Oh, yeah. Here you go." He dug into the inside pocket of the windbreaker he was wearing. "This is from my rounds the past couple of days." He pulled out a thick envelope and extended it to Lucky.

"Go on and just throw it in there." Lucky nodded toward his glove box; then Major Pain did as he was told.

"You know, for a minute there I thought one of your bitches was pulling a *Misery* on you or some shit." Major laughed. "I thought one might have had you tied up somewhere holding your ass hostage. You know that Kat broad is crazy. I wouldn't put that kind of thing past her ass. But then she came over to Spot A lookin' for your ass yesterday. Hell, her ass know you well enough where she can do the rounds." Major Pain laughed.

Kat had been blowing Lucky's phone up beyond belief. He'd had to download this app someone had told him about that sent her calls directly to voice mail. She left him all kind of crazy and deranged messages. He knew it wasn't nothing that a nice piece of jewelry, some money to go shopping, and some dick wouldn't cure.

"Yeah, I gotta get at her before she files a missing persons report and has the cops looking for me and shit," Lucky joked.

"And you know we can't have the cops looking for your ass, so you betta handle that ho quick, fast, and in a hurry."

Lucky knew Major was right. He had to settle Kat down. She wasn't his girlfriend, but she was the main girl he knew would always be just a phone call away. But considering it had been Secret he'd just spent the last few days with instead of her spoke volumes. He thought about the prospect of perhaps Kat being replaced as his go-to, keep this one around chick. He shook his head and bit his bottom lip while thinking, *Over her dead body*.

"No license?" Lucky said to Secret as they stood in front of a nice little BMW that the salesman who had been helping them asked if they wanted to test drive. Lucky couldn't believe his ears when Secret told him she couldn't test drive the car because she hadn't yet gotten her license.

The way Lucky was looking at her made Secret feel stupid. She began to tuck her head away as if she were a turtle going back into its shell. "I'm sorry. I just never . . . My mother never . . ." Secret couldn't even find the right words. Her focus had been so tough on getting out of Flint, that she didn't even consider her means of transportation.

"It's cool, baby," Lucky told her. "I ain't have nobody to teach me how to drive either. I taught myself. Owned a car and was driving for four years before I ever got a license."

Secret quickly looked up at him. "I don't want to drive without a license. I don't want to get in trouble."

"We have a company we refer people to that gives driving instruction," the salesman interrupted and said. "It's not that expensive. For now, even if you just pass the written part, you can get your temps." He did not want to lose this sale, and was therefore willing to do whatever it took to help this couple decide to purchase the BMW.

"Well, figure that out later," Lucky said. "For now, I'll test drive it and see if it's a car a chick can handle." He smiled and winked at Secret.

A half hour later, after test driving the car, Lucky was laying enough cash in front of the salesman to close the deal on the BMW. Secret just sat there amazed when Lucky went to his glove box, pulled out an envelope, and gave most of it to the salesman.

"For now we'll just put it in my name," Lucky told her. "As soon as you get your license, we can transfer the title to yours."

Secret just nodded, still not able to believe this dude she had only known two weeks had just purchased her a car. Shawndiece was going to be so proud, or hating on her, considering she had screwed so many dudes and hadn't even gotten one to buy her a moped.

"Shawndiece got a license, right?" Lucky turned and asked Secret.

"Yeah."

"Cool. I'ma bring y'all back up here so she can drive the BMW off the lot. You sign up for them classes and then . . ." Lucky stopped mid sentence. "Naw, I know your girl Shawndiece gon' be like she can teach you how to drive for less than some driving school."

Secret laughed at the fact Lucky already knew her friend so very well in such a short period of time and not even having been around her that much. That's exactly some stuff Shawndiece would say.

"So, I'll just throw her a couple bills and she can teach you or whatever."

"Trust me, Shawndiece will be down for that." Secret felt confident that her best friend could teach her how to drive; after all, she'd pretty much taught her everything else.

Lucky and Secret left the salesman's office after finalizing all the paperwork. Once they got back in Lucky's car, Secret called Shawndiece, who agreed they could come pick her up and she'd drive the BMW back to the hotel. She also agreed to teach Secret how to drive for a few dollars. Shawndiece was ecstatic about the whole car situation. She was more excited than Secret was. This reminded Secret of what her grandmother used to tell her about when you really love somebody.

"When you really love somebody, or when somebody really loves you," her grandmother had said, "you can each celebrate one another's success."

This was just more proof that Secret really didn't need to know that Shawndiece was truly a real friend.

"What she say?" Lucky asked Secret after she ended the call with Shawndiece.

"She's all for it; just like I knew she would be."

"Yeah, I figured she would be. I know her kind."

Secret turned and looked at Lucky with offense. "What's that supposed to mean?"

Lucky could tell by Secret's tone she hadn't liked his last comment.

"Oh, nothing, baby girl. Calm down. It ain't no dig against your girl. It's just that, I hate to say it, but Shawndiece is your typical hood chick. I don't mean that in a bad way. It just means that she's gon' get hers by any means necessary." He shrugged. "And if you ask me, ain't nothing wrong with that. It's called survival. Hell, it's the hood motto. So relax, baby girl. Shawndiece is good with me."

Secret was glad Lucky had explained himself. Shawndiece was one of the most important people in her life and it appeared as though

Lucky was going to become a close runner-up. All of a sudden Secret's belly got jittery, like she had to throw up. She grabbed her stomach and kind of hunched over.

"You okay?" Lucky asked.

Secret shook her head. "I think I'm about to be sick. Maybe you should pull over."

Lucky pulled off to the side of the road. No sooner than Secret opened her door did she throw up. Lucky handed her a napkin out of his center console. Secret wiped her mouth and then sat back in the seat, closing the car door.

"You okay?" Lucky asked her.

"Yeah, must be something I ate." Secret knew exactly what it was. It was her baby correcting her statement; letting Secret know that it was the most important person in her life. That both Shawndiece and Lucky were the runners-up.

Point taken, baby, Secret thought. *Point taken.*

"Do you think you might need to go to the doctor's or something?" Lucky asked with a look of concern on his face.

"No, I'll be . . ." Secret thought for a moment. Her going to the doctor would be the perfect opportunity to get the ball in motion for her plan. But did she really want to go through with this plan? This wasn't who she was. Actually, due to circumstances, this was who she had to become. "As a matter of fact, I think I might need to do just that." Secret smiled inside as Lucky pulled off. The ball was in motion all right. It was just a-bouncing indeed. Now she just had to wait to see where it would land.

Chapter Twenty-two

"Pregnant?" Lucky couldn't believe his ears. He sat in the hotel room, on the couch next to Secret. She was staring at him, trying to see if she could read his emotions. He wouldn't look at her, though. He just looked straight ahead. He washed his hands down his face and then still just looked straight ahead.

"I'm sorry," Secret finally said. She was sorrier than Lucky would ever know. She was sorry for the huge lie she was about to live with this man.

"Are you sure?" was all Lucky said, still not looking at her.

Secret got up and went to the bathroom. A few seconds later she returned with some sort of stick in her hand. She extended it to Lucky. He looked at it for a moment. He looked up at Secret for the first time and then looked back down at the stick. He took it from her hand and then studied it.

"Pregnant," he read the message on the rectangular caller ID–type screen on the stick.

"And that's the second one. Shawndiece and I bought two just to be sure. Both read that I was pregnant."

Secret hadn't made the doctor's appointment she'd told Lucky she had after he suggested she go see the doctor. He was genuinely worried a couple days ago after he had to pull over to the side of the road for Secret to throw up. She didn't need to go to the doctor's because she knew exactly what was wrong with her. But she also needed proof, which was when Shawndiece informed her that it was cheaper to stop off at CVS and pick up a couple pregnancy tests than it was to visit a doctor with no insurance. Secret knew Lucky would have paid for the appointment, but she was already doing him wrong. She didn't want to do any extra if she didn't have to. Secret had already gone to the free clinic and they'd confirmed her pregnancy with both a urine and blood test, so that wasn't an option.

"Pregnant," Lucky said under his breath again. He stared down at the results on the stick. "Pregnant." It was clear he was having a hard time dealing with the reality Secret had presented him with. "Man, I didn't see this coming." He continued shaking his head.

Secret had a feeling things weren't going to go so well. There wasn't an ounce of excitement in either Lucky's voice or his eyes. "Yes, I'm pregnant."

Lucky looked at her for what seemed like forever. "Are you ready to be a mother?"

Secret's eyes got big. What exactly did Lucky mean by that? Shawndiece had warned Secret that the first thing Lucky would probably ask her was how much she needed for an abortion. She had been schooled how to answer that question and the series of others that would be the follow up. But this question she hadn't prepared for? Was it some kind of trick question?

"I, uhhh . . ." Secret was stumped.

"Or did you wanna get a . . . you know . . ." Lucky allowed his words to drop off, hoping Secret would pick them up. Any other chick, or at least any of the others he'd gotten knocked up, already had their hand out for the amount of money they would need for the abortion as well as what they'd need from him for pain and suffering. He had to keep telling himself though that Secret wasn't those other girls. Therefore, he needed to handle things differently with her than he would with the next chick.

Okay, here it comes, Secret thought. This was the path Lucky would try to take that Shawndiece had warned her about. It was time for the detour.

"I hate to say this, but I'm so glad my grandmother isn't here to see me right now. She'd be so disappointed," Secret started. "This isn't what she wanted for me. Let my mom tell it, my grandmother used to be a force to be reckoned with, but that's not the grandmother I knew. The grandmother I knew raised me in church and taught me all the Christian values she thought I'd need to survive the pull of the streets." She looked up at Lucky with tears in her eyes. "I'm sorry I brought all of this on you. But to answer your question, no, I'm not ready to be a mother and I know you're not ready to be a father. I should have thought about that before I had unprotected sex with you. Yeah, you could have used a condom, but I should have been on the pill. I should have at least told you that I wasn't on the pill."

Secret swallowed and then hurried to continue her spiel just like Shawndiece had told her to do. She was not supposed to let Lucky get a word in edgewise until she was finished with her entire speech. "Fornicating and getting pregnant I'm sure has my grandmother rolling over in her grave. And even though I'm not ready to be a mother, that's exactly what I'm going to have to be. I'm not going to add sin on top of sin by killing my baby through abortion." She squeezed the tears out of her eyes. She then touched Lucky on the cheek. "But what I'm not going to do is force you into being a father."

The look of shock on Lucky's face let Secret know she had him just where she wanted him. So she went on. "The last couple or so weeks of my life, Lucky, have been . . ." She stared off as if she were reminiscing about a trip to Disney World as a child. "It's been like a fairytale, and that's all because of you. You are right; no one, man or woman, has treated me the way you have treated me. Has made me feel the way you have made me feel. And this child I'm carrying"—she rubbed her stomach—"will forever be a reminder of that."

Secret sighed and turned away. "Shawndiece is going to drive me downtown tomorrow to get the ball rolling with getting on public assistance. I'm going to look into government housing as well. Shawndiece said until I get set up with a place, I can stay with her. And don't worry; I'm not going to name you as the father on the birth certificate or anything. That way they won't try to come after you for child support. I'm going to take responsibility for this." Secret paused. The ball was now in Lucky's court.

"Damn, I don't even know what to say. I'm like four, five years up on you, yet you sitting here ready to take on more responsibility than I could have ever dreamed of doing." He chuckled. "Hell, you got a nigga all fucked up. Not just with the situation, but with the way you ready to hold the situation down solo."

Secret didn't respond. She just let him continue to dribble the ball.

"I'ma keep it one hun'id with you; I had no idea where this thing with you was headed. I just know that I was feeling you and really enjoyed your company. And you right; it's been like a fucking fairytale for real. I ain't never picture me giving so much time to no chick. But with you . . . it's just crazy. Not sounding like no pedophile or child molester, but I've really felt like a father running home to see his little girl. And please don't take that the wrong way, 'cause I don't even get down like that."

Secret smiled her understanding of what he was trying to say.

"But a baby." He shook his head. "Damn, Secret. I can't even say that's what I see in my future with you."

Secret's heart dropped. She knew Lucky was about to drop her. He was about to call her bluff by sending her packing to Shawndiece's house.

"So even though a baby is not what I see in my future with you," Lucky continued, "Looks like, regardless, that's what the future holds, because as foul a nigga as I might have ever been in my life, I ain't never gon' be one a mutherfucker can say didn't take care of his seed." He put his hand on Secret's stomach. "I just hope it's a boy."

Secret was elated at Lucky's reaction to the news that he was about to become a daddy by a girl he'd just met. And now it was time for Secret to be honest with herself: this was no longer just all about the baby. She was falling hard for Lucky. He always told her how different she was from other girls. Well, he was different from other guys, at least, the ones she'd heard about or met through Shawndiece. Everything in Secret wanted to get up and do the Holy Ghost dance like they used to do at her grandmother's church, but instead she just broke out in tears while thinking, *Slam dunk! It's on, baby!*

Chapter Twenty-three

"Your pussy must be lined in gold!" Shawndiece said as she walked in the hotel room and high-fived Secret.

"Girl, I thought I was going to fall out and die. I was literally holding my breath to the point I was about to pass out." Secret put her hand on her chest. "When I told that man I was pregnant, I thought it was game over before we even got to half time."

"Bitch, I told you it was all going to work out." Shawndiece sucked her teeth. "Ye of little faith." She strolled over to the mini fridge. "What y'all got to snack on?" She opened the fridge and pulled out a chocolate pudding. She peeled the foil back on it and began eating it with her index finger. "Come on, trick, so we can go practice driving. I ain't gon' be driving you and some crying-ass baby around."

"Girl, you have had free rein of a car you don't have to pay for and half put gas in. You should be grateful whether you driving just me or me and a baby."

Shawndiece stopped and thought for a moment. "Yeah, you right. My bad. Get yo' shit. Let's go."

"Hold on, heifer." Secret chuckled as she went in the room to get her shoes and purse.

"Hurry up so when we get in the car you can tell me the whole scoop, word for word, what all he said."

Shawndiece had been taking Secret out for driving lessons in the parking lot of a closed-down store. Being the wiz Secret was, she'd already passed the written exam and had her temps. She caught on to things quickly and realized it would only be a matter of time before she aced this driving thing.

After Secret practiced driving for about an hour, the two went and picked up a copy of Secret's birth certificate. Shawndiece told her she was going to need that in order to sign up for welfare. Secret carried her social security card in her wallet, so she was good on that end.

The girls headed down to the welfare department with all the documentation they thought Secret might need in hand. After almost four hours of signing in, filling out an application, and being interviewed by a case worker, Secret was approved for a medical card, food stamps, and a monthly check. When Lucky extended Secret's stay at the hotel, he put the room in her name. She was basically considered homeless, so her case worker saw to it that she received emergency and immediate assistance. She also gave Secret the information she would need to get emergency housing assistance as well.

Three weeks from the date Secret told Lucky she was pregnant, she had a driver's license to drive her car on her own, an apartment in a pretty decent neighborhood, a fridge full of food, and had gone to her first prenatal appointment. She learned that she was around eight weeks pregnant. With the due date her doctor had given her, the math would be easy for Lucky to do to figure out that Secret had been pregnant for at least two or three weeks on the day he met her, let alone had unprotected sex with her.

Shawndiece had taken the documentation from Secret's prenatal appointment to her mother's hair salon.

"Hey, ma," Shawndiece greeted her mother as she entered the shop. Secret was on her heels.

"Hi, Miss Franklin," Secret said to Shawndiece's mother.

"Ma, I need to use the copy machine in your office right quick," Shawndiece said, as she kept walking toward the back of the shop where her mother's office was. "And you got any Wite-Out?"

"There some in the middle drawer of my desk," her mother returned. "Oh, yeah, hey, Secret."

Secret waved and followed Shawndiece back to her mother's office.

"You bring that due date paper in with you didn't you?" Shawndiece threw over her shoulder as she went and opened the drawer and pulled out the Wite-Out.

"Mmmm, hmmm." Secret handed her the paper.

Shawndiece went and made a copy of the paper on her mother's printer that served as a fax and copy machine as well as a scanner. "Here you go." She gave Secret her original back. She then began whiting out something on the copy she'd just made. She picked up the copy and began to blow the Wite-Out dry. Once it was dry she grabbed a black pen off her mother's desk and began to write something on the copy of the due date paper. She stopped momentarily and began counting on her fingers and in her head. She then continued writing.

Secret just stood there watching Shawndiece do her thing.

Next, Shawndiece took the copy and duplicated it on the copy machine. Before removing the freshly made copy, she took the original back out of Secret's hand and the copy she'd just made a copy of from off the glass of the copy machine. She then began ripping them both into shreds and then pitched them into the garbage can.

"What are you doing?" Secret asked in confusion as she watched Shawndiece.

"Getting rid of any evidence that might come back to haunt your ass." Shawndiece got the copy from the copy machine and then handed it to Secret. "Wah la." She held her hands out.

"How many times do I have to tell you it's voila?" Secret corrected and rolled her eyes, allowing them to land on the piece of paper Shawndiece had just handed her.

Secret's eyes grew as huge as saucers as she read the paper. "Girl, you changed the due date."

"Yep. Just in case Lucky wants proof; you've now got it." She pointed to the trash can. "And we've gotten rid of anything else that might say otherwise. Just don't let that nigga go to none of your doctor's appointments with you and you should be all right."

Secret looked up from the paper at Shawndiece. "Girl, with all these skills you got, surely you can put it to use somewhere and make you some real money on your own. I mean, Shawn, you are the Queen of Scam."

"Yeah, I should start charging hoes on how to get money from these sorry-ass niggas. Take one-third of their earnings like a lawyer or some shit." Shawndiece laughed.

"I can see your office sign now," Secret added. "Office of Shawndiece Franklin: Don't be the ho, be the pimp. Learn how to ho your pimp." Secret laughed.

"And you just remember that you're my first client. So when Lucky start breaking you off an allowance or something, which he will in lieu of child support, don't forget my cut."

"Trust me," Secret said, looking down at the altered paper, "you have earned it."

They exited the office, said their good-byes to Shawndiece's mother, and then Secret dropped Shawndiece off at her house before heading back to her house.

Secret was glad she had her own place now, but she had to admit that she missed having maid and room service at the hotel. No, she wasn't packing up to head off to college. Yes, she was shopping to decorate a nursery instead of her college dorm. Still and yet, she wasn't under her mother's roof having to deal with the likes of all her "I told you so's."

The good thing about the situation Secret found herself in was that Lucky was taking good care of her. The bad thing was that the honeymoon was over and she didn't see as much of Lucky as she did when she was staying at the hotel. She hoped that would all change once she had their child.

"Our child," Secret spoke between her lips as she ran her bathwater. The fact that she was starting to believe her own lie scared her. This was no more Lucky's baby than it was the man on the moon.

As she began to peel off her clothes to take a bath after her long day with Shawndiece, Secret stared at herself in the bathroom mirror. Guilt took over her. Not just the guilt of the scheme she was running on Lucky, but the guilt of the fact that she was in complete bliss.

"Oh God," she said to her reflection in the mirror. "I'm happy. I'm in total bliss. But how can I be so happy knowing I'm doing something so wrong? Knowing I could ultimately hurt someone?" She looked down at her baby bump.

Secret's mind began to assault her conscience. Yeah, she was getting away with murder right now, but what about the future? What if all of the lies came back to haunt her?

"Everything done in the dark comes to light," her grandmother once told her, even showed her a scripture in the Bible that confirmed it.

Hearing those words play themselves over and over in her mind, as far as Secret was concerned, was like a warning that eventually all of this would catch up with her.

She envisioned her and Lucky at the altar about to say their "I do's." As soon as the preacher summoned anyone to speak as to why the two should not be wed in holy matrimony, someone would stand and confess Secret's dark secret on her behalf. She envisioned the baby getting sick and needing a blood transfusion or something. When Lucky would go to give blood the doctors would inform him that the baby couldn't possibly biologically be his.

Then what? What would Secret do? What would Secret say if any of this ever came to pass?

Then the big one crushed down on her conscience like a shoe coming down on a roach once the kitchen lights in a roach-infested home got turned on. How would this affect her baby? Lucky might run out on her, leave her standing at the altar, but he'd more than likely leave the child as well . . . just like her father had left her.

It would be a vicious cycle, a family curse, repeating itself over and over and over again.

"No," Secret said to herself, shaking her head at her reflection in the mirror. "I won't let you do this."

"Won't let who do what?"

"Arrrrgggggg!" Secret screamed out at the startling deep voice. Between the bathwater pounding into the tub and her drowning in her own thoughts, she hadn't even heard Lucky enter the home. "What are you doing here?" Secret hadn't expected to see Lucky for a few days. He'd already been by to check on her twice that week. Three times in one week would be a first.

"A nigga can't stop by and check in on his baby mama?" He kissed her on the cheek. "Damn, you sexy as hell pregnant." He eyeballed her naked body.

Secret immediately grabbed a towel and covered herself up with it. It wasn't as if Lucky hadn't seen her naked before, it was just that this time she felt exposed, exposed in a different way. This time she felt as if he could see right through her nakedness and down to her soul . . . her lying-ass soul.

"So you talking to yourself now?" Lucky asked her. "I be away from you that long that now you talk to yourself?" He placed a hand on each of Secret's shoulders and turned her toward him. "I can't have that, now can I? Which is why I have a special treat planned for you." He looked over at the tub. "Hop your ass in that tub, get to smelling all good, put on something sexy, pack an overnight bag, and then meet me downstairs." Lucky kissed Secret on the forehead and went to exit the bathroom.

"Lucky, wait . . . what . . . what's going on?" Secret asked, not sounding excited at all, more like burdened.

"I said I got something special for you," Lucky told her.

She didn't deserve it is how Secret felt. She did not deserve Lucky and she sure didn't deserve whatever it was he had all planned out for her. She was a fake, a phony, and a liar. This wasn't who she was. The real Secret was kind, honest, and loveable. Who wouldn't love and want to be with somebody like that? With that being said, Secret figured if she revealed her true self to Lucky, he would have no choice but to still love her. To still want to be with her. He might not want to claim her baby as his own, but that would be something she'd just have to live with. What she couldn't live with was this lie eating away at her.

"Before we go to do this surprise or whatever," Secret said to Lucky, "can we talk first? There's something I need to tell you."

Chapter Twenty-four

"Ta-da!" Lucky opened his arms wide after removing his hands from in front of Secret's eyes.

Secret stood in the middle of a romantically decorated penthouse suite. Her mouth dropped open as she admired the dozens of vases full of roses that filled the room. She admired the tall stick candles in crystal candle holders that sat upon the counters, and the variety of chocolate-covered strawberries. There were trays of fruit, cheese, crackers, veggies, and meats. There was a tray of different kinds of sushi and sauces. There was champagne as well as nonalcoholic champagne. There was a basket of various massage oils, tools, and toys.

"Lucky, I . . ." Secret was speechless as she looked around. What should have made her feel like a queen only made her feel worse than she had before leaving the house.

Now more than ever she wished she'd gotten everything off her chest before she and Lucky had left her place to head to her surprise.

He had just looked so happy and elated about whatever it was he had in store for her that she couldn't bring herself to burst his bubble with the famous Maury Povich line: "Lucky, you are not the father." So, "We'll talk later," was what she said instead, as he drove her about thirty miles outside the city to the hotel she now stood in.

"I just wanted to do something special for you is all," Lucky told her as he sat on the couch and then patted the spot next to him for her to come and sit down.

Secret slowly walked over and joined him, her stomach feeling sick inside, having nothing to do with the precious life that was growing inside of her, but everything to do with her deceit that was, too, abiding within.

"You surprised?" Lucky said, putting his arm around her.

She nodded.

"Good, 'cause I know I ain't been there like I was at first. I'm working hard, building an empire for my little prince or princess." He placed his hand on Secret's stomach. "I'ma keep it real with you, Secret." He looked around the room. "I'm trying to create this fairytale for you. But in real life, I'm a grimy-ass nigga. There's just something about you, though, that makes me want to be better. I know that might sound all soft and shit, but for real; I like who I am when I'm with you. I've never met a chick like you, ever. Most chicks always trying to run game, a gold digger or just on some grimy scheming shit her own damn self. But I knew you weren't that type of breed from the moment I saw you. I ain't never said this to no broad in my entire life. Not only have I never said this to no broad, but I've never felt it. But, Secret . . ." Lucky gathered his words as if contemplating whether to say them. "You the first chick I can actually trust, and that goes for my mama as well."

As sweet as Lucky's words were, to Secret they were like nails down a chalkboard. How could she have let Shawndiece talk her into this? How could she not have thought about the consequences and who might get hurt in all this? Now here Lucky thought she was some saint. Surely she was going to go to hell for this.

"I just want to let you know," Lucky continued, "that no matter what ever happens with us, you've shown me that there are some good women out there who aren't always out to get a nigga. I just thank God He sent you to—"

"Stop it! Just stop it!" Secret shouted as she stood up from the hotel room sofa.

Lucky was startled by her abrupt reaction. "What is it? I'm sorry. I hope you don't think I'm just talking shit, you know, shooting game. 'Cause I'm for real, Secret." He stood up and walked up behind her. He didn't touch her. He just stood there.

"I know you mean it, Lucky." Secret closed her eyes and shook her head. "That's the problem." She turned around to face him. "I know you have been nothing but genuine, honest, and have meant everything you've said to me from day one."

Lucky put his arms around Secret's waist. "And you mad about that. Hell, I thought that's what chicks wanted out of a guy."

"It is. I do, but . . ." Secret tried to turn away from Lucky but he gripped her waist and wouldn't allow her to.

"Don't turn away." He examined Secret's eyes. "What is it?" He looked down at her stomach. "Is it the baby?"

Secret's eyes began to water. "No, yes. I mean . . ." Secret managed to pull and back away from Lucky.

"Oh God. Is the baby okay?" Lucky came toward her again with a look of great concern on his face. He'd witnessed a lot on the streets.

People getting hurt, wailing in the valley of the shadow of death, some not so lucky in life as to cheat death. Hell, he'd been the causing factor in deaths. So Lucky didn't easily get moved by tragedy. Hell, his life had been a tragic tale itself as far as he was concerned. But the thought of something tragic happening to his seed brought out a whole new emotion in him he'd never experienced before.

"Did you find out something from the doctor or something?" Lucky tried not to sound shaken, but he was. "Is the baby going to be born okay? Is the baby still alive? You didn't miscarry did you?" Lucky just kept shooting out the worst thoughts that were going through his mind. "Is the baby going to be healthy? Is it going to have that Down syndrome thing or something?"

Secret watched in horror as Lucky went through an array of emotions. Guilt was overtaking her. Up until now she had been able to wash traces of guilt away with thoughts of the baby, but she'd already come to the conclusion that it wasn't all about the baby anymore. She'd caught feelings for Lucky. She cared about him. She didn't want to hurt someone she cared about. She didn't want to be that person. She didn't want to be the person she was trying to be on purpose: a deceptive liar. She just began to shake her head, silently telling Lucky no to everything he was asking. No, she couldn't do this.

"Is the baby developing okay? Is it two babies? Is the baby—"

"No, no, no," Secret began to shout, still shaking her head.

"Then what is it?"

"It's not yours!" were the next words that flung out of Secret's mouth. She wished she could have stopped them in mid air, then sucked them back in, but it was too late. They'd already reached Lucky's ears as he stood there, stunned. "The baby . . . it's not yours, Lucky," Secret admitted, not able to go on with the charade any longer. It was just too much. *All dark things come to light.* Her grandmother's sayings kept haunting her. Well, she wasn't about to let her dark deed come to light. She was going to turn on the switch herself.

"What? What the fuck did you just say?" Lucky asked in a menacing tone. This was the first time that side of him had shown itself around Secret. And right about now, if she'd said what he thought she'd said, he wasn't going to try to hide it.

Secret hesitated. Lucky had never used that tone with her and she didn't know if she was pushing her luck by continuing. But she'd pretty much already crossed a bridge; it was too late to avoid what awaited her on the other side. So she kept walking. "Lucky, I'm sorry. You are not the father of my baby." Secret had already confessed the worst. It only made sense for her to continue with the whole truth. "I . . . I was already pregnant when you met me. That day you met me at the clinic, that's what I was there for. I was there to get a pregnancy test. It was positive. I was already almost a month pregnant when I met you. So in all actuality, I'm two months pregnant right now . . . not one."

Lucky remained silent, a menacing look on his face to match his earlier tone.

Secret just hoped all that remained menacing about Lucky was his tone and that he didn't snap off on and put his paws on her. "I don't know who the father is. I don't know who the father is, not because I'm some ho and slept with a lot of guys, but because I had to sleep with one guy in order to save my father's life. And I'd rather not know who he is." Secret began to relay the horrible story to Lucky about how she'd waited for her father to come visit her. How all she ever wanted was to be daddy's little girl. How once he finally did show up, it was only to use her. She tearfully and painfully spoke about the transaction that started in a back alley and ended with her having sex for the first time in her entire life with a complete stranger; all in the name of love for her father.

Once Secret finished her story, she waited for Lucky to reply. His few seconds of silence were deafening. They felt like forever until he finally cleared his throat and spoke.

"So this has all been a game to you? Some setup?" Lucky breathed in and out through his teeth with tightened, round lips. He had no idea he was doing the Stevie J from *Love & Hip-Hop Atlanta* rat face.

"No." Secret held her hands up in defense. "I was feeling you that day at the bus stop. Really I was. I knew deep down inside I was going to call you; just not so soon."

"Oh, yeah, that's right; you were going to wait a week to call me." Lucky looked at Secret knowingly. He recalled in their very first conversation where she mentioned she hadn't wanted to call him so soon; that she'd wanted to wait at least a week so he wouldn't think she was a bugaboo.

"No, not that week crap. That was just some slick line I was feeding you when I first called you. I'd planned on waiting way longer than a week. I'd planned on waiting until after . . ." Secret's words trailed off.

Lucky shifted from his left leg to his right to let Secret know he was waiting for her to finish her thoughts. Here all along he thought she was different than all those other hood rat gold diggers out there. Ironically, she came with a bigger agenda than any of them ever had. And hers was hidden. As least with the around-the-way girls he knew exactly what he was getting. They wore their intentions on their sleeves so that there was no confusion. But this one, this chick who stood in front of him, she'd pulled the ultimate whooo whammy on him.

He'd never been so glad in his life he'd kept his and Secret's relationship on a low. He would get clowned by all his boys if they knew that he had been . . . well . . . clowned. *I should have treated her just like the last bitch,* he thought. Had he done just that, there would have been no love lost. But now, a month in dealing with Secret, and he was feeling a certain kind of way. He obviously was still feeling a certain kind of way or he wouldn't have just been standing there waiting for an explanation from Secret. He would have been done rose up and moved on to the next female. But here he stood . . . waiting.

Secret swallowed hard and then continued. "I wasn't going to call you until after I'd gotten the abortion." Secret put her hands on each side of her stomach. It was as if she was covering the ears of her baby so that it couldn't hear its mother's initial intentions for it. "But I was going to call you. I liked you. Then when I did call you and spent time with you, I liked you a lot. A whole lot. I know it's only been a month, but being with you has felt like a lifetime. I've been waiting for someone to make me feel that way since my grandmother died. And just now, sitting on that couch, I felt . . . I felt . . ." She took a deep breath. "I know it's too soon to say it, and I know it probably doesn't exist. But it's what I felt. Love is what I felt, Lucky. You made me feel love."

Lucky watched as Secret stood with tears pouring down her face. She was like this sweet, innocent, hurt, little girl. He wanted to reach out to her. His pride wouldn't let him though. She'd fooled him up to this point. For all he knew, she was still playing him.

"That's why I had to tell you the truth. I couldn't sit there and let you waste all that on me. All of whatever it is that you're giving me. Maybe it's not love. Maybe you're just running game too. Hell, I don't know. All I know is that either way it goes, I don't deserve it. You don't deserve this." She raised her hands and let them fall to her side. "I'm sorry, Lucky. I'm so sorry. If I could do it all over again I wouldn't have even taken your number. I would not have called you, not until I'd dealt with my situation. But I was desperate. I didn't know what to do. But what I did know was that if I was going to keep this baby, it would need a father. I was just so scared." Secret shook her head. "I didn't mean to drag you into this, Lucky, and I'm so sorry I did."

Secret was pretty much out of words to say. So on that note she picked up her purse and her suitcase, then headed to the door. She put her hand on the knob. Before opening the door she turned to Lucky and said. "I am really sorry. I just didn't want to do this by myself." Secret pulled the door open.

"You don't have to."

Lucky's words almost scared her. He'd been silent, so his deep voice penetrated her sharply. Secret turned and looked at him. "Wha . . . what did you say?"

Lucky put his hands in his pockets and then looked downward. "You said you didn't want to do this by yourself. Well, you shouldn't have to." He shook his head as if unscrambling the words he was trying to get out. He looked into Secret's eyes. "You don't have to. You don't have to do this by yourself."

Secret wiped her tears away. "What do you mean?" She needed clarity.

"I'm sorry. I'm sorry this happened to you. Yo, that was a fucked-up predicament your pops put you in. I can only imagine that some shit like that would make somebody do something desperate. And your moms not being there to support you . . . I know how it feels not to have anybody to support you. I don't even blame you. I guess we just all products of our environment. But this one . . ." He walked over to Secret and put his hand on her stomach. "This one won't be; not if I can help it."

Secret was tired of Lucky playing with his words. She needed him to come out and say exactly what he meant by all this. No reading between the lines. She needed it in black and white. "What are you saying, Lucky?"

"I'm saying that you had a plan and we gon' stick to it."

Secret's eyes widened. Was Lucky saying what she thought he was saying?

"We gon' finish what you started. Only now I guess I'm in on it too. As far as anybody is concerned, that's my baby you carrying."

"Lucky," Secret said, finally able to exhale. She buried her face in her hands as tears poured out. "I don't know what I ever did in life to deserve this. To deserve you," Secret's muffled voice stated.

"Don't go making it seem like I'm some saint or something. I'm far from that." Lucky shook his head thinking about his past and some of the awful things he'd done. "I wasn't able to save a lot of my homies. In some cases I was probably the downfall of a couple of 'em. So maybe with this here baby it's like God is giving me another chance to save somebody. And, I promise, I won't fuck this one up." He removed Secret's hand from her face. "Don't cry," he told her as he took his index finger and caught one of her falling tears. "Daddy's here." He knelt down and kissed her pregnant stomach. "Daddy's here."

Chapter Twenty-five

"Girl, if I had been there I would have straight pulled that nigga's thug card," Shawndiece teased as she and Secret talked on the phone.

Secret had just gotten back home and settled from her night with Lucky in the hotel suite. She had spent the last few minutes relaying to Shawndiece everything that had gone down.

"Girl, it was so sweet. I thought he was going to cry," Secret said.

"'When Thugs Cry,' ha, that's gon' be my new anthem for that nigga. I swear if we ever out and around his boys, I'm gon' clown his ass good." Shawndiece was cracking herself up.

"Well, you can file that under never. I've never even heard Lucky mention any of his friends' names, let alone meet any of them."

"Word?" Shawndiece was now in serious mode.

"Yeah." This was something Secret hadn't really thought about until now.

"What about his family, his moms or any-body?"

"He did mention his mom and dad once; the fact that they were drug addicts and in jail or something like that."

"Oh, well, the story of a thug." Shawndiece sighed. "But still, I know with the type of business he's in, he got at least one or two flunkies or sidekicks."

"Like you know what Lucky does for a living."

"Like you don't," Shawndiece shot back. "Girl, don't try to play naïve and stupid. The fact that you haven't straight-out asked that nigga exactly what he does for a living and the fact that he hasn't straight out told you speaks volumes. But you playing your cards right by not asking. The less you know, the better. Which is probably why you've never met any of his boys. You different, Secret. I've always told you that. Lucky can see it too. He knows better than to taint you with the cats he rolls with. You ain't about that life. It would be like mixing oil and water. You wouldn't fit in and his boys would clown him for even fucking with somebody like you. Or they'd think he was plain stupid and getting played."

"Why, is that what you think about him?" Secret decided to finally interrupt Shawndiece and speak.

"Well, uh . . ." It was far from usual for Shawndiece to ever be at a loss for words. "I mean, no, because you my girl and I know your heart. I know you really didn't want to go into this to trap old boy out of malice or to just be stank. That's what God put me on this earth for." Shawndiece let out a chuckle in which Secret joined her subconsciously. "But for real, I saw how you was feeling Lucky from the moment you met him. You had every intention of calling him up. After all, your initial intentions were to get rid of the baby, so it wasn't like you were going to get with dude thinking a baby would be in your future."

Secret loved the fact that Shawndiece was lifting some of the thoughts that had been burdening Secret about being with Lucky. She couldn't help if he wondered or doubted her wanting to be with him because of who he was and not what he could do for her and her baby. Hopefully he could see down to her heart just like Shawndiece and know that she really liked and cared about him.

"You watching an episode of *Scandal* you done recorded or something? Because you sho'nuff is ignoring the fuck out of me," Shawndiece barked through the phone.

"Oh, huh, what?" Secret said, snapping out of her thoughts.

"Nothing, girl. I'm gon' let you go. Bitch tired as hell. My cousin Rah-Rah wanted this expensive-ass sew-in weave that had my black ass up until the wee hours in the morning finishing up. And I was s'posed to hook up with Paco tonight but I'ma have to call him and postpone. You know a bitch tired if she passing up getting her pussy ate right and a shot at that new Michael Kors bag from Macy's."

"Girl, bye," Secret said, hanging up the phone in Shawndiece's ear, never amazed by what came out of that girl's mouth.

Secret let out a yawn, too. She was tired as well, as she should have been from making love to Lucky all night. She decided to lay it down for a nap. Her ringing cell phone woke her up out of her sleep two hours later.

"Hello," Secret answered groggily.

"What's up with my baby mama?" Lucky spoke.

"Oh, hey, Lucky." Secret stretched. "What's up?"

"Nothing, just handling some business. You sound tired."

"I was taking a nap."

"Oh, my bad, I didn't mean to wake you up."

"It's okay."

"Well, I ain't gon' keep you. I just wanted to let you know that I dropped a li'l somethin'-some-thin' in your bank account. You was acting all shy and crazy about me seeing your naked body all last night."

"'Cause I got that baby bump now." Secret touched her belly.

"Girl, I told you nobody can't even tell you're pregnant. But since you think you getting all big, I put some money in your bank account so you can go shopping for some bigger clothes."

"Awww, baby, thank you." Secret smiled. This type of thing didn't even surprise her coming from Lucky. He was just that kind of guy who never had to ask or guess at what she wanted or needed. He just knew.

"No problem. Well, go on and lie back down. I'll holler."

"All right. Thanks again."

Secret ended the call and then lay back down. She closed her eyes but then they popped back open after only a few seconds. "Who can sleep when there's shopping to do?" She laughed and hopped up out of the bed. She went to the bath-room, washed her face, and brushed her teeth. She put on eyeliner, lip liner, and lip gloss. She wasn't that big on makeup, but Shawndiece insisted she do a little something to remove herself from Plain Jane status. She was actually going to call Shawndiece to see if she wanted to roll with her, but remembered Shawndiece saying how tired she was. She was not trying to get cursed out by calling and waking her up. Secret got herself together and went shopping by herself.

After two hours of nonstop shopping, Secret had worked up an appetite. She decided to go the Chinese restaurant located in the strip mall. Although she didn't feel like dining in, she figured she would go inside to place a to-go order.

With a couple shopping bags in hand, Secret made it to her car and added them to the collection that was already forming in the trunk. She was a few stores down from the restaurant so she got in her car to drive over. While heading toward the restaurant she saw a male figure enter the restaurant. She was still quite a few feet away, but she'd know her baby daddy anywhere.

"Perhaps I will dine in." Secret smiled as she began her search for a parking spot. While driving down one aisle, Secret saw Lucky's car parked in the lot, more confirmation that the man she saw entering the restaurant was him.

After finding a spot Secret got out of the car and started walking toward the restaurant. The parking lot had been pretty full so she had to park farther away than she would have liked. As she got closer to the restaurant, she saw another gentleman coming from the opposite direction, looking as if he was headed toward the restaurant too. Secret fell back a little bit, realizing she and the man were going to arrive at the door at the same time. She'd allow him to be the gentleman and go first, hopefully opening the door for her.

The closer Secret made it to the restaurant, the more excited she was about her chance impromptu meeting with her baby daddy. She just hoped she was able to catch him before he ordered carry-out so that they could dine in together.

With a huge grin on her face, Secret was prepared to enter the restaurant. The kind gentleman was, in fact, standing at the door, holding it open for Secret.

"You coming in here?" he asked as Secret made it just one foot from the door.

Secret, for the first time, actually made eye contact with the guy. Upon doing so, she couldn't speak. She just shook her head no to his inquiry and kept walking. She picked up her pace, practically running. Her breaths became deep and long to the point where it was like she couldn't remember how to exhale. She just kept walking. She had no idea where she was walking to; she just knew where she was walking from.

When Secret decided she was going to go into the restaurant and have a sit-down meal with her baby daddy, she had no idea she was going to actually run into him. But she had. She'd recognize that face anywhere. The man who stood there holding the door for her was the man from the alley that night. The memory of that night came flooding back to her. Shame filled her being. Standing before her was the man she'd paid her father's debt with her body. The man who took her virginity. The man who she was now pregnant by. Yes, it was true; Secret had definitely just run into her baby daddy . . . her real baby daddy!

Chapter Twenty-six

"What up, pa'tna?" Major Pain said after spotting Lucky over at a table by the window in the Chinese restaurant he and Lucky had agreed to meet up at.

"Nothing," Lucky said, staring out of the window with a confused look on his face. "I thought I just saw somebody I knew walking by."

"That shit must be going around, 'cause I thought I just saw a familiar face as well. Some chick I hit a couple months back as a pay off from some geeker." Major Pain sat down. "Although I wouldn't mind hitting that shit again. Running up in her felt like the first time I'd ever run up in some pussy in my life. All brand new and shit." He grabbed his manhood up under the table. "Make a nigga wanna go out there and chase her ass down just thinking about it." He laughed. "Bitch probably wouldn't give me the time a day. She didn't seem like all these other hoes we be fucking wit'."

"Enough talk about old pussy. Let's talk about new business," Lucky said. He looked at his watch. "By the way, you late, nigga."

"Man, fuck you. I know you ain't talking shit. The same nigga who is like the fuckin' black James Bond nowadays. One minute you here and one minute you there and shit." Major Pain picked up a menu and began to scan it. "Anyway, what's up?"

"Motherfucker! I done caught up with yo' black ass now. You can run, nigga, but you sho' the fuck can't hide."

Lucky closed his eyes and put his head down at the sound of the distant familiar voice that was getting closer until it was right up on him.

"What up, Kat? You lookin' your regular hood-fabulous, loud-ass ghetto self today," Major said once Kat approached the table.

"Fuck you, Major. Don't fuck with me," Kat spat. She slammed her hands into her hips and then turned to face Lucky. "Really, Lucky, it's like that?"

"Oh, shit." Lucky washed his hands down his face. He had a look on his face as if he'd just remembered something he'd neglected to do.

"Yeah, that's right, motherfucker. You was supposed to hook up with me yesterday." She began making quotation marks in the air and mimicking Lucky. "I got something special planned for you. I know I been fuckin' up, but just let me make it up to you." Kat slammed her hands down on the table causing those patrons who had tried to play it off and ignore her rant to give their table their full attention.

"Come on now, Kat. You see a brotha taking care of business here." He extended his hands in the direction of Major Pain.

"Business, business, business," Kat mocked. "That's always your excuse. For years you've been playing me like some dumb-ass ho. Well, not anymore, Lucky. This is the last mother-fuckin' time you will ever . . ."

Kat went on and on and on nonstop. Her voice was giving Lucky a headache. He just wanted her to stop. He wanted her to go away so he could handle his business at hand with Major Pain. The more Kat talked, the more aggravated he got. But she was on a roll. There was no stopping her. She wasn't coming up for air. Lucky tried to find a place to jump in, but Kat wouldn't allow him to get a word in edgewise. Finally he just snapped.

"Look, ho, you know what it is. You ain't new to this shit so stop acting brand new. Now get the fuck out of here embarrassing yourself and me."

Kat was taken aback. Sure Lucky had talked mad shit to her in the past. She'd taken it just as good as she'd given it. But there was something about his tone this time that told her things had changed, and not for her good.

"Ohhhh, I get it," Kat said as if coming to a revelation. "You real brand new. I mean for real, coming at me like that, you acting real brand new right now. And there's only two things that make a nigga get all brand new. That's either new money or new pussy. And since money ain't a thang to you, it must be new pussy. Is that what it is? Some bitch got your nose wide open?"

Lucky didn't deny it. He just looked away. When he saw that Major Pain was staring at him, waiting on him to respond, he tried to play it off by sucking his teeth and shooing his hand. "This bitch crazy," he hissed.

"Crazy for always being there whenever you've wanted or needed me." Tears formed in Kat's eyes, which shocked the hell out of Lucky. He'd seen Kat cry before, but usually it was out of anger. Usually she was mad because he had her in a bear hug or something to keep her from swinging on him. She'd be angry that she couldn't lay hands on him. She'd get over it and then afterward they'd have good old-fashioned makeup sex. But this time Kat's tears were different. They weren't tears of anger. They were tears of pain, and something told Lucky there would be no chance of makeup sex . . . ever.

"I can't even believe I actually really cared about yo' ass," Kat said as a tear spilled from her eyes. She tried to wipe it real quick, but it was too late. She'd actually allowed Lucky to see her shed a tear over him.

"Like I said, you know what it is. Now me and my boy here need to talk." And just like that, Lucky dismissed her. His ride or die chick. His bottom bitch. His down-ass chick. It was done and over with. Lucky could just tell, so there wasn't no need in him trying to make nice and promising her a purse, pair of shoes, or tennis bracelet. He had to admit, pre-Secret he probably would have entertained Kat's rant, given her some money to go shopping, and then hooked up and fucked the shit out of her later that night. But now he felt he didn't need to. As far as he was concerned, he'd found him someone to add to his circle that would be genuinely down for him no matter what he did or didn't have to offer.

"So that's all you have to say to me?" Kat said in disbelief that Lucky was so quick to send her on her way. When Lucky, once again, let his silence do his talking, Kat let out a "Fuck you!"

Before anyone could stop her, Kat had picked up one of the cups of the complimentary tea the restaurant provided and splashed it on Lucky. Fortunately for him, it had been sitting there long enough to cool off so it didn't scorch him or anything. Unfortunately for Kat, it still pissed Lucky the fuck off. So much so that he jumped up, his hands in position to snatch Kat up by the throat. Major Pain was just as quick and able to get in between the two. By that time the manager, who had been off to the side watching the showdown, finally got the balls to come interfere.

"You no fight in here," the Chinese man squawked. "You leave now or I call police." He was directing his words to Kat as he took her by the arm. He knew better than to throw his regular, paying, high-tipping customers, Lucky and Major Pain, out of the restaurant. Their regular business meetings over lunch damn near kept the lights on in the joint. But Kat he had no problem kicking to the curb. Literally.

"Get the fuck off of me," Kat spat to the manager, snatching her arm from his grip.

The manager didn't use his hands, but his body to kind of push and escort Kat toward the exit door. She screamed and hollered the entire way.

"You're dead to me," Kat screamed and pointed at Lucky as the manager kept using his body weight to push her toward the door. "I don't even know your name anymore. You don't even deserve for your name to come out of my mouth anymore. For now on, I'm just gon' refer to you as L. Not for Lucky, but for Loser, you son of a bitch. I swear to God I will never say your fuckin' name again. I never knew you. This is the last time I'ma ever let you play me for a fool. You're dead to me, L. Dead!" That was the last thing Kat spat out just as the manager pitched her out on the sidewalk and closed the door.

Lucky wasn't even embarrassed that he'd just been caught up in such an outburst. He was used to this type of drama, damn near immune to it. Lucky picked up the other cup of the complimentary tea the restaurant served. With his pinky in the air as he took a sip he looked at Major Pain and then said, "Back to business. Now where were we?"

Chapter Twenty-seven

"Katherine? Katherine, is that you?" Secret said. Could her eyes be deceiving her two times in a row and within minutes? They couldn't have been. Just like she'd know the face of the man who fathered the baby inside her belly, she'd definitely know her sister when she saw her, even if it had been years since she'd last seen her. But she'd know Rolland's eyes anywhere. Her sister—legally half sister since they only shared one parent—had their father's eyes.

Secret called out to her again; still the girl didn't even flinch. Secret knew it was her, but she was torn between going to try to have a conversation with her and keeping it moving. Instead of walking on the sidewalk and crossing in front of the Chinese restaurant and risking her real or fake baby daddy seeing her, she'd cut into the parking lot and was dipping and dodging between cars. Every few seconds, as she passed the Chinese spot, she looked to make sure neither man was exiting. In doing so, she spotted Katherine stomping across the lot.

As the girl kept walking across the parking lot toward Secret like she was Oprah Winfrey in *The Color Purple,* Secret thought perhaps she was mistaken. After all, she was standing right in her path, calling out her name, and the girl wasn't flinching. But the closer the girl came the more sure of herself Secret became.

"Katherine? Katherine," Secret called out. The girl's eyes saw right past Secret and smoke could have been coming out of her ears. It was clear to Secret that her sister was in her own world, oblivious to her surroundings. "Kathy!" Secret yelled once she saw her sister was actually going to walk right by her.

The girl's four-inch stilettos could have left skid marks as she came to an abrupt halt. "Huh, what?" The girl's eyes began to focus in on Secret. She tilted her head from the left to the right.

"Katherine, it's me, Secret. Rolland's daughter. Your baby sister," Secret said, practically pleading for this girl to remember her.

"See-See," Katherine said, using the nickname she'd called her when they were little girls.

"Yes, it's me, See-See," Secret said.

"Oh my God!" And just like that, Katherine's angry scowl was replaced by complete joy as she threw her arms around her sister's neck, her sister she hadn't seen in practically a decade. "I can't believe this." She pulled back and gave Secret the once-over. She then pulled her into a tight hug again. "I can't even believe this."

"I know, right," Secret said, returning her sister's hug.

Katherine released her once again. "I feel like I'm on some *Color Purple* Celie and Nettie shit," Katherine joked.

"Well, just a minute ago you was on some Miss Sofia stuff," Secret joked. "I thought you was going to stomp right over me."

"Oh, girl, that's because I just almost caught me a case. I just had to cancel somebody out of my life. But look at God. I get rid of one person and just like that"—Katherine snapped her fingers—"He put somebody else in it. And not just somebody else. My sister." She looked Secret up and down. "Wow, See-See, I still can't believe it's you. You all grown up."

"You too." Secret looked Katherine up and down. She noticed her designer jeans, her bedazzled tank top, and stilettos. She also peeped out her nice jewelry and designer Ralph Lauren leather purse. Secret had to keep from laughing. If it wasn't Katherine's face, she'd have sworn up and down she was staring at Shawndiece.

"How are the twins?" Secret asked. "I know they are grown."

Katherine rolled her eyes and sucked her teeth. "Grown and gon' end up in jail if they don't stop trying to be some wanna-be gangstas. Out here gang bangin' and shit." She shook her head. "Just hardheaded. But what do you expect when they ain't got no daddy in their life. Speaking of daddy, have you talked to our sorry-ass daddy?" Katherine asked Secret.

"Umm, no," Secret said, realizing that she was nodding her head yes. "Well, uh, not in a minute. How about you?"

"Not since he showed up for my eighteenth birthday. I'm thinking this nigga coming through to finally act like a real daddy. His ass was just tryin'a see what I got for my birthday so he could get me to pawn it. I cussed him the fuck out. Then he got to talking about how he had this huge debt and they were going to kill him if he didn't pay them off, blah blah blah. Some old jive-ass game he was running."

Secret was all too familiar with that game. "So did you pawn anything for him?"

Katherine rolled her eyes in her head. "Girl, yeah." She broke out laughing. "What can I say? He's still my pops and I guess I'm still trying to be daddy's little girl. I ended up letting him pawn my iPad and iPod. Girl, not the new ones I got on my birthday, but the old ones that the ones I got for my birthday replaced." She chuckled. "I might be some dumb, but I ain't plum dumb. I knew that jive-ass nigga ain't owe nobody no money. He just wanted to get high is all. I vowed after that, after I let my own pops play me, that I'd never let a man play me like that again." All of a sudden Katherine stopped talking, that scowl returned to her face as she looked over her shoulder back at the restaurant. "'Cept when it comes to Lu . . . I mean L, for loser."

Katherine turned back around to face Secret. "But I don't want to talk about that. It's water under the bridge." The smile returned.

"Well, we are going to have to get together sometime," Secret suggested. "Maybe we can grab a bite to eat."

"Sure, we can grab a bite."

"Cool." Secret smiled, then thought for a minute.

"But not in there!" they both said simultaneously, referring to the Chinese restaurant. Both girls burst out laughing.

"Guess you ain't in the mood for Chinese either," Katherine surmised. "Anyway, I'm parked right there." Katherine pointed to a royal blue Toyota.

"I'm over there." Secret nodded to her vehicle.

"Wanna hit that Applebee's around the corner?" Katherine asked.

"Sounds good to me." Secret grabbed her stomach. "And this baby."

"What? You prego. OMG, See-See." Katherine went and touched Secret's belly. "You can't even tell. But you can feel."

"Yeah, I'm just a little bit pregnant."

"Just a little bit?" Katherine laughed. "You crazy. Anyway, I'll meet you over there and you can tell me all about baby and your baby daddy." Katherine paused. "You still with the baby daddy?"

Secret's face lit up. "Yes, I am."

"Oooooh, and I can tell by the look on that face that he must be handling his business. You lit up like a light bulb."

Secret nodded proudly. "Yeah, he takes good care of me, that's for sure."

"Good. Well, you can tell me all about him while we eat. I need to live vicariously through some other happy couple right about now seeing I'm about to cut men off period."

"Okay. I'll meet you there," Secret said before making her way to her car and heading over to Applebee's. She couldn't wait to catch up with Katherine and rekindle their sisterhood.

Even more so, she couldn't wait to tell her just how lucky she was, and she meant that literally considering she was about to tell her all about Lucky.

"Okay, so tell me all about this baby daddy of yours," Katherine said to Secret after they put their drink orders in with their waitress. "Is he fine?"

"He's easy on the eyes," Secret said in a modest tone while blushing.

"What's his name?" Katherine asked. "You know Flint ain't but that big." She snapped her fingers. "I probably know him. But then again, look how long it's taken me to run into you. What's it been like ten years?"

"Yes, just about," Secret confirmed. "We should have looked each other up long before now."

"Yeah, I know." Katherine lowered her head in regret. "But we've found each other now. And you are right on time. I had been dealing with this dude, who shall remain nameless, because like I told him, he's dead to me. His name doesn't even deserve to be on my tongue, let alone his dick."

Secret practically cringed in embarrassment.

"Oh, shit, did I say that as loud as I think I did?" Katherine put her hand over her mouth.

"Uh, yeah, you did."

"My bad."

Secret smiled. "You know, you remind me so much of my best friend. You two are going to get along just fine. I have no doubt about that."

"I don't know, looking at you Miss Thang and listening to you talk . . . Not trying to be funny, but you kind of like a white girl trapped in a black girl's body. Seems like your best friend's name would be Amanda and she'd carry her dog named Fe Fe in her purse."

Secret laughed along with Katherine.

"Why does everybody say that about me? That I'm different? Like I don't fit or something? My baby daddy is forever saying stuff like that." Secret's face lit up. "He tells me I'm nothing like the girls he's used to dealing with." Secret shrugged. "So, I guess I better start taking what all y'all are saying as a compliment."

"Even when we were younger, and even though I was only around you a few times, I knew you were different from all the other girls I knew, different from all my cousins and stuff. That's why when my moms used to bad-mouth your moms I knew she was just jealous that pops was hittin' both of them at the same time. There was no way something as evil as my mom claimed your mom to be could have produced someone as nice as you."

Secret put her hand up. "Whoa. Hold up. Don't go giving Ms. Yolanda too much credit now. She can be a beast."

Katherine thought for a minute and then shooed her hand. "Hell, we all can be. That's how bitches get when they dealing with losers. Trust me. I just got rid of my L; loser." Katherine used her index finger and thumb to hold up the L sign. "I don't care what no muthafucka says; behind every angry black woman is an asshole of a man who made her that way."

Secret laughed. "Yes, indeed, I can't wait for you to meet Shawndiece." Secret took a sip of her water. "Or my baby daddy for that matter." She rubbed her belly.

"Oh, yeah, back to him," Katherine said. "You never did tell me what Prince Charming's name is."

"Oh, it's—"

"Have you two had a chance to look over the menu?" their waitress returned and interrupted.

"Oh, shoot, not yet," Katherine said. She looked at Secret. "Girl, let's stop running our mouths long enough to see what we want to put in them." She looked back at the waitress. "Just give us five more minutes, I promise."

"No problem," the waitress said and then walked away.

"Get anything you want," Katherine told Secret. "It's on me . . . I need to drown my pain in hot wings and a margarita."

"Don't' worry, sis. It's going to be all right. God doesn't make mistakes. Obviously ol' dude's time in your life has expired and it's time for you to move on. Before you know it, you'll find somebody new and forget all about that joker." Secret scanned the menu.

"Yeah, you right." Katherine sighed. "And if I'm lucky, I'll find a man like yours who makes my smile light up the room at just the mention of him."

"Yeah, maybe," Secret bragged. "Maybe."

Chapter Twenty-eight

"It's a boy," the nurse said as she pointed out the baby's genitals on the ultrasound screen.

"I'ma have me a nephew in three months?" Shawndiece yelped. "Oooooh, I can't wait to buy him some Nikes. As a matter of fact, I think Footlocker got baby Nikes on sale. I should go ahead and cop them now."

"Girl, you're going to start spoiling him while he's still in the womb?" Secret said as the nurse wiped off the jelly she'd placed on Secret's stomach for the ultrasound. "Besides, don't think you're going to turn my baby into a label freak. Remember, I know how low some of the folks around these parts will stoop for a name brand." She shot a knowing look at Shawndiece.

As far as Shawndiece was concerned, Secret might as well had said the words "hint, hint."

The nurse looked up and eyeballed Shawndiece in the midst of the now-awkward silence.

"What?" Shawndiece threw her hands on her hips like she was offended. Secret was too busy looking at the still image on the screen to notice her best friend's reaction to her comment.

"Uh, are you good on your prenatal vitamins?" the nurse asked Secret.

"Oh, yes. I think the doctor gave me enough refills to last me throughout my pregnancy," Secret replied.

"He usually does. I was just making sure," the nurse said. She pitched the paper towels she'd used to wipe off Secret's stomach into the trash. She then headed back to the ultrasound machine and handed Secret a few pictures of the baby she'd printed off.

"Thank you so much." Secret admired the pictures as if she was looking at her child's first picture day in kindergarten.

"Do you have any questions or need anything else?" the nurse asked.

Secret shook her head.

"Then I guess we'll see you next time." The nurse headed toward the door. "Don't forget to stop on your way out to schedule your next appointment."

"I won't," Secret said, sitting up. "Thanks for everything."

"No problem." The nurse smiled as she exited the room, closing the door behind her.

Secret sat up and pulled her shirt down over her belly. She just sat there for a moment staring off. "A little boy." A smile graced her face. "Although the sex didn't matter, I'm so glad it's not a girl. The last thing I wanted was for her to turn out like all the other chicks in the neighborhood." Secret slid off the table and grabbed her purse. "You ready to go?" she looked to Shawndiece and asked.

"Am I ever," Shawndiece spat, cutting her eyes at Secret and then brushing past her out the door. She almost ran into the nurse who was headed back into the examination room.

"I almost forgot," the nurse said. "Here's that prescription for the new iron pill the doctor is going to try you out on. Hopefully this one won't constipate you as much."

"Oh, thank you," Secret said, taking the prescription.

Secret went and scheduled her next appointment, then headed toward the exit doors. Shawndiece was keeping pace at least ten feet ahead of Secret.

"Dang, wait up," Secret called out to Shawndiece as she exited the doctor's office.

Shawndiece stopped and waited until she felt Secret next to her, never looking over at her or making any type of eye contact.

"I can't believe I got a little boy growing inside of me," Secret said as she tried to keep pace with Shawndiece across the parking lot. "I just wish Lucky had been here to witness it." Secret started to look a little gloomy.

Shawndiece stopped in her tracks, turned to face Secret, and grabbed her by the shoulders. "Look, bitch, this ain't la-la land and it sure the fuck ain't no fairytale. Quit acting like you thirty years old with a husband, a dog, and a cat, about to have your first child. You in Flint, nigga. You living in a subsidized living joint in the hood. Ain't no nice pretty house on the hill surrounded by a picket fence. And the man who agreed to claim your child as his own ain't even the real baby daddy. He out hustling and grinding so that you don't have to want for nothing. So stop your whining, take that nigga a picture of that little jelly fish of a baby, suck his dick, say thank you, and keep it moving." Shawndiece released her with a slight push, and then kept walking.

Shawndiece had just burst Secret's happy balloon wide open. She knew she wasn't living society's version of a fairytale, but somehow, in her own mind and in her own make-believe world, she was living the life closest to a fairytale she might ever have. She didn't need for Shawndiece to be yapping off at the mouth trying to rain on her parade.

"You think you know everything," Secret shot back at Shawndiece. "And you think you can just talk to people any way you want to," Secret shouted out to her as Shawndiece kept on walking. "Well, bitch, fuck you!"

Shawndiece stopped in her tracks and turned around. To Secret it was as if Shawndiece was turning in slow motion.

Oh, shit, was what popped up in Secret's head. Had she really just gotten fly at the mouth with her best friend who she knew she couldn't go toe to toe with on a good day?

"Oh, you got courage now, huh?" Shawndiece said. "You done visited Victoria's Secret and bought and put on some big-girl panties. Now you ready to rumble. Or either you think just 'cause you got a bun in the oven you can talk crazy to me and get away with it." Shawndiece balled a fist and said through gritted teeth, "Girl, you think I won't fight nobody pregnant?"

Secret remained silent. She didn't want to piss Shawndiece off any more than she already had.

"Now that the little game you were playing with that nigga Lucky is over and you done got what you've needed out of me. You and Lucky about to live happily ever after so you just gon' shit on me? You gon' talk shit to the bitch who is the reason why your situation is going good?

If it wasn't for me, you'd been sitting up in an abortion clinic somewhere and living with your mean-ass mama."

"Oh, so you trying to say I'd be like you?" Secret had done it again. She'd snapped off at Shawndiece. She wanted to instantly recoil, but instead, she poked her chest out and her six-month belly. For years Secret had let people say whatever they wanted to say to her just because they thought she was weak. It was a shame that just because she chose to speak proper English, cover her body with clothing, and not let every other word that flew out of her mouth be "nigga" or a curse word that she was weak. Well, for once it was time she stood up for herself, even if it had to be against her best friend.

Secret's words had cut Shawndiece, but that didn't stop Secret as she kept on turning the knife. "Is that what you're mad about? That you been tricking niggas for years and ain't got nothing to show for it, and you mad that I ain't you, running around on the lookout for niggas to sponsor me? I done told you, Shawndiece. I've told you, my mother, and everybody else: I'm not going to be you! I'm not going to be them! I'm going to be better. I'm going to make a better life for me and my baby."

Shawndiece paused for a minute. "So I wasn't hearing shit up there in the doctor's office, all those submental messages you were throwing?"

"What?" Secret had an annoyed look on her face. "You mean subliminal?"

"Bitch, you know what the fuck I mean. You always correcting somebody like you the smartest motherfucker on the planet. Yes, subliminal messages. I heard your little shots you were taking at me up there. Talking about how low people stoop for name brands and how you glad you're not having a girl so she won't be like me."

"I didn't say that," Secret said.

"In so many words you did."

"I didn't mean to say it like that, but guess what, Shawn, it's the truth. I want my baby to be better than you and me."

"But especially me, huh?"

There was silence. Shawndiece took Secret's silence as a yes. "Good, I'm just glad you could use the little people like myself to get where you need to go in life." Shawndiece shook her head. "But just know from this point on, I'm done. You on your muthafuckin' own." Shawndiece threw up the peace sign. "Deuces." She then walked off.

After taking a few steps Secret called out to her friend. "Shawndiece!" Her plea was ignored. "Shawn, get back here. I drove, remember?"

Shawndiece stopped and turned around again. "I'm gon' catch the bus. Maybe I'll be so lucky as to meet my thug in shining bling while waiting at the bus stop just like you did." After her sarcastic statement she was off again.

Secret just stood there in regret. She knew Shawndiece better than anybody. Once her best friend was done with somebody, she was done. Secret could only pray that she'd make an exception for her. After all, she might have thought that the game might have been over, but the score clock was still ticking.

Chapter Twenty-nine

"What the fuck? You for real?" Lucky roared into his cell phone. He was sitting in the passenger's side of Secret's car. She was driving them out to a restaurant. For the first time since they'd been together, Secret had actually talked Lucky into letting her take him out and treat him to dinner. It was a special night Secret had been looking forward to all week. It was extra special because she hadn't laid eyes on Lucky all week. She'd talked to him on the phone, but that wasn't the same. She hadn't seen Lucky in four days straight. It was special for Lucky, too, as no broad had ever offered to buy him a meal—even cook him one for that matter.

After a few minutes of them being in the car, Lucky's phone had rung. He ignored the call and put it on vibrate. By the assigned ring tone, Lucky knew it wasn't anybody but Major Pain calling him. He'd call him back as soon as he had a chance to talk outside the presence of Secret. Lucky was good for sending his calls directly to voice mail when he was with Secret. That's exactly what he'd done at first. But Major Pain had been calling him back to back and then finally sent him a text that read:

911. Pick up, Nigga. Dope Boy got shot.

"Hell yeah, I'm for real," Major Pain replied from the other end of the line. "And he had just delivered the shit and was about to make the drops. I'm headed to the hospital now. So you know what that means. You gotta go get that shit. It's too much going on right now. You know we can't trust none of them other cats right now. We down a soldier and mutherfuckers' minds is preoccupied. That's the perfect scenario for a ma'fucker to get caught slipping. The twins and Devon at the spot now, but I don't trust them niggas to the degree I want them to handle that. You feel me?"

"Yeah, yeah, I'm on it," Lucky replied.

"All right, nigga. One." Major Pain ended the call.

Lucky tucked the phone in his pocket and just sat there looking panicked and concerned.

"What is it? Who was that?" Usually Secret never questioned Lucky about anything. What she didn't know could never hurt her; at least that's what Shawndiece, her best friend she hadn't talked to in a month, had taught her. But this time things just sounded too serious for Secret to ignore. "Lucky, what's going on?" Secret asked after he failed to reply to her first inquiry. She rested her hand on his knee.

Lucky looked up at the highway exit signs. The next exit would be only about ten minutes from the spot where he needed to pick up the dope that Dope Boy would have distributed to the houses. His first dilemma he had was that he'd made it a rule to never ride dirty. He paid cats to do that. The second dilemma was that Secret was not only with him, but she was the one driving. Sure the latter could be resolved just by him having her go back to her house so he could get his truck that he'd left parked there. But that was all the way across town, at least a half-hour drive, then another half hour back to the spot. Too much stuff could go down in an hour. Too much was at stake. He and Major Pain ran an empire and trusted each other 100 percent to make sure things were run right. He couldn't let down his boy, but more importantly to Lucky, he couldn't let down himself. He had a reputation to uphold and more money to make.

"Fuck," he yelled, pounding his fist on the dashboard.

"What is it, baby?" Now Secret had fear in her voice.

"I need you to get off at the next exit." He pointed to the exit that was coming up in just a few feet.

"Why, baby? That isn't the way to—"

"Please, Secret," he yelled. "Just take the fuckin' exit," he shot off, nervous she would miss it if she didn't hurry up and do as he said.

Secret quickly whipped the car across two lanes, ignoring the horns beeping at her. She managed to make the exit. With eyes full of fear she asked, "Where am I going? What's going on?"

"Just follow my directions. Please don't ask me any questions. Just be quiet and drive," Lucky pleaded.

"Okay," was all Secret said as she stared ahead, following Lucky's instructions as if he were a GPS, navigating her to their destination. Just as Lucky had asked, she remained silent. The true test of just how silent she could remain, and for how long, was about to confront her face to face.

"I'm sorry about all this," Lucky said as he got back in the vehicle after stopping off at a house in a neighborhood Secret wasn't familiar with.

"It's okay," Secret said, the first words she'd spoken in the past fifteen minutes. As bad as she wanted to question Lucky about the huge duffle bag he'd just thrown in her trunk, she didn't. She just prepared herself to follow his next set of instructions.

Not five minutes after pulling off, Secret looked through her rearview mirror to see a set of flashing lights atop a police car. "Look, Lucky, the police."

Lucky snapped around so quick to look behind him, it was a surprise his head hadn't spun right off his shoulders. "Oh shit. You have got to be fucking kidding me," he said, then turned back around to face ahead. "They must have been watching. Fuck! Fuck! Fuck!" With each expletive, Lucky's fist pounded the dashboard.

"Baby, please calm down," Secret begged. "Don't worry. I'll pay for the ticket if I get one. He might not even give me a ticket. He just may warn me or something for whatever I did. But I didn't do anything." Secret's nervousness was reflected on each word she spoke and the speed at which she spoke them. Secret began to look for a place to pull over.

Lucky looked over to the driver's side and grabbed the wheel on instinct as if he was trying to keep her from pulling over.

"What are you doing?" Secret asked.

What was he doing was the million dollar question Lucky wanted to ask himself. Secret was a down-ass chick, but she was no Bonnie to his Clyde. His instinct was to snatch that wheel and tell her to keep driving, to outrun the police, but he knew she wasn't that type of chick. Had that been Kat in the driver seat, the chase would have been on. But it wasn't Kat. It was a seven-month pregnant chick who didn't have the street smarts to get out of a jaywalking ticket.

"Nothing, nothing. Just pull over," Lucky told her.

As Secret pulled over to the side of the road Lucky thought about the fact that as long as Secret kept cool, everything would be just fine. She was young, innocent, and none the wiser of what was actually in her trunk besides a spare tire. She wouldn't draw any suspicion and they'd be on their way.

After a couple of minutes the officer approached the driver's side of Secret's car. She rolled the window down and greeted him.

"Hi, Officer. Was I speeding?" Secret asked.

"No, ma'am, not at all," the officer replied. "License and registration please."

"Oh, yes, certainly." Secret dug down in her purse for her license and retrieved the registra-

tion out of her glove box. All the while the officer
eyeballed Lucky.

"Don't I know you from somewhere?" the
officer asked Lucky, who hadn't looked up at
the officer at all.

"Oh, Officer, please, you're actually going to
try to hit on me in front of my girl?" Lucky joked.
Believe it or not, he did manage to pull a laugh
out of the officer.

"Here you go, Officer." Secret interrupted
the little joke fest by handing the officer the
requested documents.

The officer looked over the documents. "See
here lies the problem." He waved the registration. "The name on the registration, which is you
of course, doesn't match up to the name when I
run these plates."

"Oh, shit!" Lucky said under his breath and
started shaking his head. This drew both Secret's
and the officer's attention.

"What is it?" Secret asked Lucky.

"Babe, when we got the car put in your name,
I forgot to put your new tags on," Lucky said, still
shaking his head, wishing he could kick himself
for making such a stupid mistake. Giving the
police any reason to pull over a vehicle he was in
was a stupid mistake.

"Where are they?" Secret asked.

Lucky nodded backward. "In the trunk. I can switch them out as soon as we get home."

Secret turned and looked at the officer. "I'm sorry, Officer. The name the plates are running back to is my boyfriend." She nodded over to Lucky. "When he first bought me the car it was in his name. I didn't have my license yet, only a permit. Once I got my license we put it in my name. Just forgot to change out the tags."

"You say it's in your boyfriend's name?" the officer said, eyeing Lucky again, as if he was really trying to figure out where he knew him from.

"Yes." Secret nodded.

The officer leaned down. "Sir, can I see your ID please?"

Lucky just sat there as if he hadn't heard the officer's request.

"Lucky." Secret nudged him. "The officer wants to see your ID."

After a five-second delay, Lucky dug into his pocket and pulled his wallet out. He removed his ID, then handed it to Secret.

"Here you go, Officer," Secret said, handing Lucky's ID to the officer.

After taking the ID, the officer examined it. He looked at Lucky, then back at the ID again. Now armed with both Secret's and Lucky's ID as well as the registration, the officer excused himself, instructing Secret to wait a moment while he headed back to his car.

"Fuck! Fuck! Fuck!" Lucky spat off again once the officer was back at his car. "I can't believe I fucked up and forgot to change out those tags." Lucky kept shaking his head, tightening his lips, and balling his fist.

"It's okay, baby. He seemed like he was under-standing. At the very least, we'll just get a ticket. I don't think they will tow the car or anything. I already told you I'll pay for anything that—"

"It's not that, Secret!" Lucky snapped, cutting her off. Realizing he'd frightened her when she jumped, he toned it down a little bit. "I'm sorry, it's just that . . ." Lucky knew it was in his best interest not to say anything.

"What? What is it?" Secret felt as if Lucky knew something that she didn't, but that she should.

Lucky looked over at Secret and just stared at her. His eyes said, "Are you really that naïve? Are you really?"

"Ma'am, I'm going to ask you to step out of the car," the officer said upon his return, "and open the trunk and we can get those plates out and I can help you switch out the plates." He held up a couple tools and wore a friendly smile. "You did say the correct tags were in the trunk, right?"

"Yes." Secret looked to Lucky for confirmation. He didn't say anything. She turned back to the officer. "Yes. That would be nice." Secret went to open the door.

"Thank you, but no, thank you," Lucky chimed in. "I can do it when we get home, Officer."

"But if you have them in there now, we might as well go ahead and change them out," the officer reasoned. "The next officer to pull you over might not be as nice as me." He winked.

"He's got a point, Lucky," Secret said. Lucky didn't respond. Secret went to open the door and this time Lucky let her go. What excuse could he come up with to stop her now? The girl just didn't get it.

Secret got out of the car and escorted the officer to the trunk. "Lucky, pop the trunk," Secret called out to him. A couple seconds later, the trunk popped open.

Upon opening the trunk, Secret realized the plates were not in plain sight. She shifted the few things that were in the trunk around and couldn't find them. "Oh, no, maybe they're not in here after all," Secret fretted. She paused and thought.

"Maybe they're in there." The officer pointed to the duffle bag.

Just then Secret and the officer turned and looked behind them upon hearing the sounds of gravel popping under tires. It was another cop car pulling up behind the one who had pulled them over. Both the officer and Secret stood and waited as they saw the officer driving the car get out. After getting out of the car, the arriving officer opened the back passenger's door. He then headed toward Secret and the first officer.

Secret's eyes bucked once she saw the second police officer wasn't alone. He had a dog with him. She did not care for dogs at all.

"How's it going?" the officer with the dog greeted them. "I was just driving by and thought I'd stop and offer my assistance. Besides"—he looked down at his dog—"Booser here needs to get out to do his business." He looked up at his fellow officer and smiled.

"I'm just helping the lady here switch out her plates," the first officer on the scene replied. He then turned and faced Secret. "If we can find them."

Secret smiled, but it wasn't a real smile. She was starting to get a funny feeling about this other cop just happening upon the scene.

"Well, maybe I can help you guys find them," the second officer said. He then looked at Secret. "Ma'am, do I have permission to look in your trunk?"

Secret hesitated, but couldn't think of any reason why she should tell the officer no. Either they'd find the plates or they wouldn't. "Sure," Secret agreed.

The second officer split between Secret and the first officer. He began to shift some things around just as Secret had done. "Do you mind if I take this out?" the officer said to Secret, pointing at the duffle bag.

"No, not at all." Secret's stomach began to do flips. She wasn't sure if it was the baby or her nerves, but something just didn't feel right.

The officer took the duffle bag and threw it on the ground.

"There they are!" Secret excitedly pointed. The plates had been under the duffle bag. Good. Now they could just get those plates switched out and keep it moving.

Before the officer could pick up the plates, the dog he'd brought with him started barking and going crazy, gnawing at the duffle bag.

"Booser!" the officer shouted in an attempt to calm his dog, but that didn't work. The dog just kept going crazy, barking and trying to get inside the bag.

Both officers shot each other a look. The second officer then looked at Secret.

"Ma'am, I'm Officer Hawkins with the K-9 unit. Booser here is a dog trained to sniff out drugs. We have reason to believe drugs might be in that bag. Do we have your permission to check out the content?"

Secret felt cornered as both officers glared at her. Talk about feeling trapped between a rock and a hard place. She felt she had no other choice but to give them permission. What if she said no and out of anger they let their dog loose on her?

"Ye . . . yes . . ." Secret started.

"No!"

Lucky's loud voice came booming from around the corner. Before Secret could blink an eye, the officer's had drawn their guns and had them pointed directly at her baby daddy. While her stomach did flips and her heart practically beat out of her chest, all she could ask herself was, *What the hell is going on?*

Chapter Thirty

"Put your hands on your head," the first officer on the scene shouted to Lucky as he pointed his gun at him. Lucky slowly obliged. Just as slowly as Lucky had placed his hands on his head the officer crept over to him. Once the officer was in Lucky's face, he began moving like a ninja, quickly pulling Lucky's hands down from over his head and pulling them behind his back.

The second officer kept his gun aimed at Lucky while Secret stood frozen watching it all go down. Secret watched the officer slam Lucky against the car while he handcuffed him.

"What's got you all excited, fella?" the officer asked Lucky as he tightened the metal bracelets around Lucky's wrists.

Lucky remained silent. There wasn't much he could say for what he knew was about to go down.

"Looks like somebody doesn't want us looking in that duffle bag," the first officer said to the other one who placed his gun back in his holster, all the while never losing control of the dog.

"Well, it doesn't matter," the second officer said. "The lady here gave us permission to do so."

"And it is her car," the first officer stated. He placed his lips a centimeter from Lucky's ear and whispered, "That is, if you're still sticking with that story."

Lucky just rolled his eyes and remained silent.

Not even asking Secret a second time for permission to search the bag, operating off her initial approval, the officer with the K-9 unzipped the bag while the other kept Lucky detained up against the car.

"Well, well, well, now I see what's got your boyfriend here panties in a bunch," the officer said to Secret, as once again his dog started barking wildly.

It still didn't register to Secret exactly what was going on, not even staring down at that duffle bag full of white stuff.

"Good boy." The officer pet his dog, took something out of his pocket, and fed it to the dog. The dog lost interest in the duffle bag and began devouring the snack. "Look what we have here." He held up a plastic bag full of white stuff to his partner.

"Well, I'll be damned," the first officer on the scene said. "Who would have thought a simple case of improper tags would lead to a drug bust?"

"Drugs?" Finally Secret realized what was going on. "What are you talking about?" she asked the officer. Then she questioned the person she really wanted answers from. "What's he talking about?" Her eyes pleaded with Lucky for an answer.

Lucky put his head down as if he couldn't even bear to look at Secret.

"I'm talking about enough ounces of cocaine to keep a Hollywood starlet's party going strong for a week," the officer said. He then turned to Lucky. "Don't tell me you planned on using all this for personal use," he sarcastically said to Lucky.

"No," Lucky finally spoke. "'Cause it ain't mine."

The little smirk on the officer's face disappeared. He looked over at his fellow officer with worry, then turned his attention back to Lucky. "Wha . . . what did you say?"

Lucky took a deep breath, tightened his lips, then seethed. "You heard me, mutherfucker. I said it ain't mine."

Now it was Secret who didn't speak. It wasn't because she didn't want to, but because she didn't know what to say. She was starting to catch on now. She realized that there were only two people in the car: her and Lucky. If Lucky was claiming that the drugs weren't his, that only left one other person to whom the drugs could belong: her!

The officer turned beet red as he used all of his body weight to smash Lucky into the car. "Look, you black-ass piece of shit," he said into Lucky's ear, spittle soaking the side of Lucky's face. "I know you're a low-life son of a bitch, but I know you ain't so fucking low that you're going to allow your pregnant girlfriend to take the rap on this one." He yanked Lucky to face Secret. "You really want your child born in jail?"

Secret locked eyes with Lucky. Inside she was wishing the officer had asked him something else. Maybe if that really had been Lucky's blood growing inside of her it would have made a difference. But it wasn't his baby. Lucky knew that and so did she.

Lucky dropped his head.

"Oh, no, you don't," the officer shouted, grabbing Lucky by the chin and making him look at Secret.

Secret stood there trembling as her mind began to foresee just exactly how things were possibly going to go down. "Lucky," she whispered, pleaded, and cried. Her heart rate sped up as she anticipated Lucky's next move.

"Yeah, Lucky," the officer continued to taunt. "You're not going to sit here and tell us that all those drugs belong to your pregnant girlfriend are you? Because unless you tell us the drugs are yours, well . . ." He shrugged. "The car is in her name. The bag was in her car. As far as we're concerned, the drugs are hers then. So either you man up or we handcuff your girlfriend and haul her and your unborn baby off to jail."

There was silence as the ball bounced in Lucky's court.

"Come on, man, really?" the cop with K-9 said. "What kind of man are you? Even if she was the biggest drug lord to ever walk this earth, even if you were a choir boy and never touched drugs a day in your life, as a man, wouldn't the right thing to do be to say the drugs are yours? Save the damsel from doing at least a ten year bid in the joint?"

Again, there was silence.

The officer who had Lucky apprehended just shook his head. "Well, it looks like you better book her," the officer said to his partner.

The officer exhaled. "Come on, Booser," he said to his dog. "Looks like we're gonna have company." He gathered the dog and took him back to the car. This time he placed him in the front passenger's seat.

Secret stood there the entire time immobile. This was not happening. It could not be happening to her.

"So these drugs don't belong to you?" the officer kept pressuring Lucky as they waited for the other officer to return.

"I said they ain't mine," Lucky replied.

"Then you're saying they are hers?" He nodded toward Secret.

Lucky stared into her pleading eyes once again. "I said they ain't mine."

"Then I guess they're hers." The officer shrugged.

"Lucky, please . . ." Secret begged as her bottom lip began to tremble. "Lucky. They're not mine. What are you doing?" Secret's shoulders began to heave as Lucky seemed unmoved by her pleas to him.

"Well, did the owner of the dope fess up?" the second officer said, returning without the dog.

"Yep," his partner said. "Looks like they belong to the little lady, right, Lucky? I mean, her car, the drugs were in a bag that was in her car."

The second officer to the scene looked at Secret. "You know you are going to do quite a bit of time for this, young lady." He looked down at her stomach. "Plan on missing that baby's first everything: first step, first birthday, first words, because it's going to be a long time before you see the light of day." With that being said, the officer took out his handcuffs.

"No, no!" Secret's instincts, for the first time since the cops had pulled them over, began to kick in. Without thinking, she went to run, but the officer was able to snatch her up quickly.

"No, stop it! No!" Secret screamed as she fought the officer as he forced her hands behind her back.

"Is that what you want?" the other cop whispered in Lucky's ear. "You're really going to let this happen to her?" When Lucky didn't answer he continued. "Look, just claim the dope and we'll work out a little something with you. Some kind of plea you know. You help us, we'll help you."

"You mean you want me to be a snitch or else you gon' put my black ass away for the rest of my life," Lucky said.

The officer feigned to be thinking for a moment. "Yeah, something like that." He snickered. "So what do you say?"

Lucky feigned to be thinking for a moment, mocking the officer, he then replied, "I say fuck you, pig."

In anger the cop slammed Lucky against the car. He took one hand and smashed the side of Lucky's face against the car. "Book her," he shouted to his partner, sure to make sure Lucky's head stayed in place so he could see Secret's arrest going down.

The officer who had Secret apprehended placed one cuff on her wrist and she about lost her mind.

"God, no! No!" she cried out as she bucked her body. "No, they're not mine. Please, Lucky, tell them. Help me. Don't let them do this to me. I can't go to jail. Please! Please!"

Through all of Secret's yelling and struggling with the cop, the officer managed to place her in handcuffs. Secret was crying so hard she was about to hyperventilate.

"You sure about this?" the officer who had Secret cuffed said to Lucky.

Secret cried out desperately to Lucky one last time. "Please. Please."

Lucky stared deep into Secret's innocent, naïve, and vulnerable eyes. He knew she wasn't cut out for jail. Hell, she wasn't even cut out for the streets of Flint, but what he had known all along was that she was loyal to a fault. Only somebody loyal would give up their virginity for a man who left her and her mother for dead. From the moment Lucky heard that story he knew Secret was someone he needed in his corner. Kat had been down for sure, but Kat's loyalty didn't rank anywhere near Secret's. Lucky knew that at the end of the day, Secret was the exact someone he needed in his life for such a time as this.

"They ain't mine," was all Lucky said as he then watched the police officer drag a shocked Secret over to his car and place her in the back seat.

"I'm going to call this in and call for towing to repo the vehicle," the second officer said before climbing into the driver's seat of the car.

"No problem," his partner spat before turning his attention to Lucky. "Got somebody to call to come pick your sorry ass up, because there's no way your shitty black ass is gon' stink up my car," the officer spat to Lucky as he removed the handcuffs from him.

"Yeah, can I go for my phone though?" Lucky asked.

The officer glared at Lucky before responding by doing a body search to make sure Lucky didn't have any weapons on him. The officer retrieved the phone and then shoved it into Lucky's chest.

Snatching the phone and rolling his eyes, Lucky punched in some numbers and within seconds began speaking into the phone. "Look, I know you're pissed," he said, "but now is not the time. Five-oh got me on the side of the road and I need you to come get me like yesterday." Lucky proceeded to recite his whereabouts through the phone and then ended the call. He then looked at the officer. "Can I at least sit in the car until my ride comes?"

"Hell no. Sit your ass right here on the curb where trash belongs," the officer spat before heading back to his own vehicle.

After about ten minutes both officers were still at the scene and Lucky stood waiting for his ride. The officer with Secret in tow had called in the incident, requested a tow truck, and had started filling out his report. The other officer was waiting for the tow truck to show up.

The officer driving Secret put down the clip-board he'd been writing on the last few minutes and put his running car in drive. He rolled down the passenger-side window and then slowly rolled up beside his partner, who was waiting with his window down. "The tow truck is about three minutes away. I'm going to go ahead and take her in." He nodded back toward a weeping Secret.

Just then a royal blue Toyota crept up behind them and parked. Lucky shot up from off the curb and headed toward the vehicle.

"He's really leaving me," Secret said out loud, although it was just supposed to be a silent thought roaming through her head. Was this real? Was it really happening? Secret turned around as best she could to see where Lucky was going. She didn't have a full vision, but she saw him open the door of a car that was parked behind her. He got in and closed the door as if he didn't have a second thought about her. Secret turned back forward and tears just spilled from her eyes.

As the car behind them slowly crept by in order to get back into traffic, Secret looked to her left. She'd wanted to lock eyes with Lucky. She wanted to look him dead in his eyes and try to read him. Was he this cold? Secret had no such luck as he was looking straight ahead with a stone face, like he couldn't bear to even look at Secret. Before the car could safely dip back into traffic though, Secret's eyes managed to lock on a sight she never expected to see: the driver. Katherine, aka Kat. Her sister.

"Oh my God." Once again the thoughts in Secret's head had escaped through her mouth. Was this nightmare really happening? Had her man just practically left her for dead and driven off into the sunset with her sister? Was this some bad joke? If so, who was in on it? She needed answers. Lucky wouldn't even look at her so she knew she wasn't going to get any answers from him, so out of instinct she began to shout out, "Kat! Katherine, wait!"

With the front driver's window being down, Secret's cries echoed into the royal blue vehicle. This caused Lucky to turn and look at Secret. He then looked at the driver and then back at Secret with a huge question mark on his forehead. His question mark, though, after looking into Secret's pain-filled and confused eyes, turned into empathy, sadness, and regret.

Even as Kat pulled off into traffic and Secret sat in the back seat of that police car, still crying and pleading through the window, Lucky just watched her until she was out of view.

Lucky hadn't meant for this to happen, but it had. He really did care about Secret, but he could not put himself in a position where he'd have to sell out his crew, especially Major Pain. He would do all he could to help Secret out, and hopefully get her to understand his reasoning and motives some day. Who knew? Maybe one day they could work things out and live that happy life he knew she wanted and deserved. But right now, that game had changed. And even though one day Lucky wanted to be a changed man, as much as he thought Secret would be the one to soften him and change his ways, he was who he was: Lucky. Literally, because the fact that it was Secret being hauled down the highway off to jail instead of him, where he could go on with life living as free as bird, made him one lucky motherfucker indeed.

Chapter Thirty-one

Every single moment of time felt so surreal to Secret. The drive in the back of the police car. Arriving at the county jail and being processed in. The strip search after she was stripped of her own clothes. Everything was surreal, right down to her donning the jailhouse garb and jail-issued flip-flop-like sandals she wore on her feet. The feet that stood in the corner of a cell she shared with several other suspect-looking women.

It was ironic that Secret had felt out of place most of her life. But right now, she didn't. Although hemmed up with the likes of prostitutes and other criminals, Secret didn't feel above them in any way, shape, or form. She never had in life. Her desire to become better than her environment, she felt, had been misconstrued by both her mother and her best friend. Her passion and efforts to get out of Flint weren't because she thought she was above the hood. In all actuality, she wanted to prove that the hood wasn't all bad. That the hood produced some amazing, smart, brilliant, and successful individuals.

Secret desired to be that living proof. Now more than ever that dream seemed so far out of reach. To Secret, it was a wake-up call that she was who she was: a hood chick. No matter how well she did in school and no matter how hard she tried to do the right thing, it was evident she was not going to get out of Flint. She didn't need any more convincing. This was where she belonged. This was who she was. She was, in fact, a product of her environment, an environment just not meant for her to escape. So she made it up in her mind that it was time to throw in the towel. If you can't beat 'em, join 'em.

Who had she been kidding all this time besides herself? Secret belonged to the streets of Flint, and now more than ever, it was time for her to start acting like it. She'd been raised by those streets in more ways than one. Gone would be the scared-looking, naïve little girl everybody had pegged her to be. From this moment on, Secret knew she'd better take everything she learned and put it to use, because life as she had wanted it to be was no longer an option. The dream was history. Time to wake the fuck up!

"Secret Miller," a guard walked up and called out. "Come with me."

Secret paused for a minute, looking around. She then stood with a look on her face that asked, "Who me?"

"You Secret Miller?" the guard asked her.

"Yes," she replied.

"Then come on. Who the fuck else you think got the name Secret Miller in here?" The guard shook her head in frustration as she unlocked the door, grabbed Secret by her elbow, and pulled her out of the cell. She proceeded to handcuff her before walking her down a hallway, through a door, then down another short hallway before stopping at a door. The guard unlocked the door then took Secret into the room.

Secret looked into the room that had about five chairs lined up in little cubby-type cubicles. Three of the chairs were occupied. The guard walked her down to one of the empty chairs and sat her down. She then removed the cuffs from Secret's wrists and walked away.

Secret just sat there looking straight ahead at the clear glass barrier that separated her from another room. After a few seconds, the door in the other room opened and in walked a familiar face.

Secret took in a deep breath and then let it go. She didn't even try to keep the smile on her inside from showing itself on the outside. When told she could make one phone call, her options were slim to none. But still, she took a chance on dialing the number of the person who the last time she saw them they were fighting.

As her visitor made her way over to the chair on the opposite side of the glass from Secret, Secret hurriedly picked up the phone so she could begin their communication, not knowing how much time she had to visit with them.

Her visitor picked up the phone on her side and spoke into it. "You been telling me since I can remember that the truth will set you free. Well, bitch, will you hurry up and tell the truth so your ass can get out of here and be free?" Shawndiece said into the phone.

The girls couldn't help but burst out laughing.

When Secret had made her one phone call, she'd reluctantly called Shawndiece. No matter how mad Shawndiece was at her and no matter how long it had been since they'd talked, she knew if anybody had her back it would be her best friend, her hood mentor, the girl who'd taught Secret everything she needed to know in order to make it this far in life. She'd always given Secret just the right advice, so when Shawndiece told Secret to drop the dime on Lucky and accept any plea deals that had to do with her testifying against Lucky, Secret should have agreed to do it. But she didn't. She didn't disagree either. Instead Secret told her best friend she'd just let go and let God, something her grandmother had taught her.

"God got many of the characters in the Bible out of situations similar to mine," Secret had told Shawndiece. "We've been doing things our way forever and it hasn't gotten us out of anything, only deeper if you ask me. So for now, I'm just going to be still and let this play out how it's supposed to. No more interfering with destiny."

It was clear, as Shawndiece sat across from Secret, pressing her to throw Lucky under the bus, that her days of navigating Secret through the tough situations in life were over. She officially now had to take a back seat. And Shawndiece, having taken on the role of Secret's hood-life GPS, felt pure guilt as she looked at her friend through that glass, locked up in jail gear. Shawndiece's eyes began to water.

"Bitch, you better not cry," Secret spat.

Shawndiece's tears immediately dried up, as her emotions switched gears. She went from feeling sad and hurt for her friend to complete shock. "Bitch, did you just call me a bitch?"

"Yes, because that's what you are acting like, a little bitch. I'm the one sitting in jail, about to give birth at any moment, and I ain't even crying. So you damn sure better not." Secret wanted to cry though; God knows she did, but she knew tears would not get her anywhere. They'd never gotten her anywhere with Yolanda, and they didn't get her anywhere with her father the night she got pregnant.

Secret blinked back the tears in her eyes and swallowed the ones in her throat. She shook her head and said, "You can't cry. You don't cry, remember. You've been my strength, my rock, for years. If I see you break, Shawn, I'm fucked."

Shawndiece regained her composure. "So you been in jail all of forty-eight hours and you hard now? Got a new vocabulary, cussing and shit."

Secret chuckled. "I always had it in me. Unlike you, I just know that there is a time and a place for everything. And this is the place where I put everything you've taught me into effect." Secret put her hand on the glass. "Shawndiece Franklin, I know now that all those years ago God placed you in my life for such a time as this. I've watched and I've learned from the best. So you know I'ma be all right in here. Right?"

Shawndiece nodded as a smile crossed her lips.

"See, that's what I'm talking about. Have a little confidence in your girl," Secret said.

After that, Shawndiece was feeling a lot better about her best friend's situation. They talked for around ten more minutes about how Secret ended up in jail and how they could possibly get her out.

"I swear to God, I'm going to do everything I can to get you out of here. I'm going to be at every court date, wherever I need to be," Shawndiece promised. "Oh, yeah, and I put some money on your books, too."

"Thank you. I hope you didn't put too much on them, because I don't plan on being in here too long. My hearing to set bail is next week." She looked down at her stomach. "Hopefully this bundle of joy can stay in the oven long enough not to be born in jail."

"This is your first offense. I'm thinking your bail won't be too bad. They might even let you out on your own recodonence."

"It's . . ." Secret started to correct Shawndiece and pronounce the word she was trying to say, but instead she just let it go and smiled. She knew what her friend was talking about. Just because she'd never spoken hood language didn't mean she didn't understand it.

"I'm sure Lucky will get me out no matter what the bail is," Secret said, still having some confidence in the man she felt walked into her life and saved her. Her heart wouldn't allow her to believe he'd let her rot there in jail. Only time would tell.

"Lucky? Fuck Lucky. Don't you take a red cent from that rat bastard," Shawndiece shot with venom. "That punk bitch watched them cuff and carry you off to jail . . . with a baby in your belly."

Secret understood Shawndiece's anger, but she was sure Lucky had his reasons. She hadn't talked to him yet, but she would definitely give him the opportunity to explain himself. She felt Shawndiece wouldn't understand, so she didn't even bother to speak on it with her. She didn't know how much longer they had for the visit, but she knew that she didn't want it to end on a sour note.

Just like she had been given a mental cue, the guard appeared, letting Secret know she needed to wrap up the visit.

"Aw, boo, I hate leaving you in here like this," Shawndiece whined.

"Trust me when I say a piece of you is in here with me." Secret tapped her chest where her heart lay beneath. "I got this."

"And I got you." Shawndiece put her hand up to the glass. Secret did the same. "Girl, let's stop this corny Lifetime movie shit. The last thing you want them dyke bitches up in there to think is that you a lesbo." Shawndiece quickly removed her hand from the glass.

"Girl, you are stupid." Secret laughed, putting her hand down too. "Anyway, keep your phone close to you and make sure you communicate with my mom."

"She been up here to see you yet?"

Secret shook her head. "I don't even know if she knows I'm in here. That's why I need you to communicate with her. I don't know whether she'll even care, but still let her know what's going on."

For the first time since Secret had left home, Shawndiece saw where maybe her friend was missing her mother, wanted her, needed her, and was perhaps a little disappointed that she wasn't there.

"Don't look so sad about your moms. It might be a good thing she hasn't been up here. The last thing you need right now is all her negative energy." Shawndiece then added, "I still don't understand for the life of me how you've been an understudy to the epitome of ghetto-hood-project chick and had to be taught by me." Shawndiece let out a tsk.

"I learned to tune out Yolanda once I no longer needed her titty for nourishment. It was my grandmother who I took after. Now that there was a lady."

"Umm, hmm, and as you know this ain't the time or the place to be a lady."

Secret smiled. "I know. Just do what I said. Stay by the phone and communicate with my mom. I'm going to need all the help I can get, even if it's from her."

"I will," Shawndiece promised. She said her good-bye, hung up the phone, and then stood. She watched her best friend be hauled off behind a huge metal door. She then turned to leave, thanking God her lone tear had waited for Secret to be out of view before it fell.

As the guard placed Secret back in the cell, Secret turned and watched the door close. A smile crept across her face as she shook her head. "Streets of Flint, you win," she said as she then looked down at her stomach, knowing that it was only a matter of time before she'd have to turn her seed over to its rightful parent as well: the streets of Flint.

"Well, little one," Secret said, inhaling new life and puffing her chest out. "Game over." She exhaled in defeat, knowing it was time to mentally prepare herself for the life she was truly destined to live. She had no idea who this new life would include. Shawndiece she knew for certain would always be her girl. Her mother was iffy, but who knew? Hearing her only child was locked up with child could soften her hard heart. Her dad was dead to her. Then there was her sister, Katherine. What was her connection to Lucky? And at the end of the day, where would Kat's loyalty lie: with Lucky or with her blood?

Last but not least, perhaps Secret's life would include Lucky, perhaps it wouldn't. Maybe he'd bail her out, hire her a high-priced, fancy attorney to get her off the hook, he would explain his actions, she would forgive him and they would live happily ever after. Or maybe he would leave her there to rot like he never knew her. Who knew? She could end up serving as the State's star witness and testifying against him so that their roles reversed and he was the one rotting away in jail. At this moment, nobody knew the answer to all that but God. It was all in His hands. The question was, could she trust Him with her life? As she stared at the door that sealed in her freedom, confining her into her jail cell, Secret knew she didn't have a choice.

ORDER FORM
URBAN BOOKS, LLC
97 N. 18th Street
Wyandanch, NY 11798

Name (please print):_____

Address:_____

City/State:_____

Zip:_____

QTY	TITLES	PRICE

Shipping and handling-add $3.50 for 1st book, then $1.75 for each additional book.
Please send a check payable to:
Urban Books, LLC
Please allow 4-6 weeks for delivery